THE BLACK BOX

By the Same Author

Fiction
Merry Town, Missouri - 1945-1948, A Novel
Out of the Riven Century, Stories
Witches of Devon, Tales

History
American Army Doctrine for the Post-Cold War
Evolution of American Army Doctrine (in *The Origins of
Contemporary Doctrine*, ed. John Gooch)
From Active Defense to AirLand Battle
Prepare the Army for War (coauthor)
The Army of Excellence
A History of Army 86

THE BLACK BOX

Darwin, Marx, Nietzsche, Freud

Stories by

Nickell John Romjue

To ANDREW and ALISON
and
To the rising generation who demand answers to
the great Why?
of the 20th century

610 East Delano Street, Suite 104, Tucson, Arizona 85705 U.S.A.
www.wheatmark.com

Publisher's Cataloging-In-Publication Data
(Prepared by The Donohue Group, Inc.)

Romjue, John L., 1936-
  The black box : Darwin, Marx, Nietzsche, Freud : stories / by
Nickell John Romjue.

  p. ; cm.

  Contents: Darwin's black box — The red priest and the actress
— Homo liberalis — Zarathustra — Love and Freud — The
mysterious stranger.
  ISBN-13: 978-1-58736-710-6
  ISBN-10: 1-58736-710-6

1. Secularism—Fiction. 2. Materialism—Fiction. 3. Philosophy
and science—Fiction. 4. Science and civilization—Fiction. I.
Title. II. Title: Darwin's black box. III. Title: The red priest and
the actress. IV. Title: Homo liberalis. V. Title: Zarathustra. VI.
Title: Love and Freud. VII. Title: The mysterious stranger.

PS3618 .O45 2006
813/.62006933780

CONTENTS

ACKNOWLEDGMENTS

GRATEFUL ACKNOWLEDGMENT IS made to the literary journals that first published several of these stories which dramatize the "Black Boxes" of the secular belief systems that proved so consequential in the history of the violent 20th century: *Shenandoah* for "The Mysterious Stranger"; *Writers' Forum* for "Zarathustra"; *Karamu* for "The Red Priest and the Actress" (under the title "Exorcisms"); *Aura Literary/Arts Review* for "Homo Liberalis" (under the title "The Shattering"). Included herein are two stories whose subject and theme, central to the intent of this book, appeared in earlier collections, *Out of the Riven Century* (2001) and *Witches of Devon* (2002).

Special thanks are again due to my wife Inge for her faithful love and support.

Cover images are used with the permission of Brown Brothers, Sterling, Pennsylvania.

AN INTRODUCTION

Stories, History, and Black Boxes

No IDEA OR metaphor more clearly explains the breakup in our time of the great secular creeds and moral notions that so powerfully and fatefully shaped the mind of the late-modern world — than the *Black Box*. The great theories and credos of nature, man, and society developed in the late 19th and early 20th centuries by Charles Darwin, Karl Marx, Friedrich Nietzsche and Sigmund Freud all contained in their visionary structure a chamber of surprises, a Black Box that the authors of those idea-systems, in their time, could not or did not see into and whose inner mechanisms were unknown and had yet to be revealed.

Today the Black Boxes have been opened. Science and history's hard lessons have laid bare their contents. From where we stand at the outset of the 21st century, the unforeseen implications of the Black Boxes have exploded the materialist belief systems of modernity's famous quartet of founders.

The stories in this collection explore those Black Boxes and their implications: the cell of life and its intricate and indisputable design, which the crude optics of Darwin's time could not penetrate; the hidden component of mass killing that proved organic to revolutionary socialism and from which Marx averted his gaze; the propensity of Nietzsche's bold vision of trans-moral *overmen* to produce not the aesthetic ideal but morally free individuals and cold totalitarian monsters; the widespread subversion of individual moral behavior legitimized by the deluded Freudian assertion of the primacy of subconscious drives over the rational mind.

To the idea of a natural world formed and constituted exclusively of the interaction of material forces that Darwin had theorized, and whose unfolding human history Marx had reduced to a materialism-centered orthodoxy of revolutionary utopian socialism — to those powerful new ideas, Freud and Nietzsche had added a further general notion fateful for the disordered era to come. Their negative achievement, each from its own vantage, was to detach from the new exclusively materialist definition of human reality the very idea that a universal, objective morality existed at all.

In the latter decades of the 19th century, influential portions of the educated classes of the United States, England, Germany, and other Western nations would — under the dominating influence of Darwinism — cease to believe in a transcendent moral law given to humanity by a Creator God existing beyond history and the material world. Succeeding generations through the 20th century would come to accept a profoundly secularist worldview, casting religion as no more than a human invention, and morality itself as a value not applicable to all humanity but relative to culture and situation.

The moral balance of the emancipated 20th century, however, would go colossally wrong. The new secular faiths grounded in a world of matter alone would powerfully influence new ideologies-in-power gestated in the cauldron of the First World War. Out of the new ideologies of Communism and National Socialism would come new, *unGodded* power regimes that assumed to themselves the mantle of higher morality. In the 20th century, the higher morality of Nazism and Communism would kill its racial and class enemies — men, women and children — by the scores of millions in Eastern Europe, Soviet Russia, Communist China, Vietnam, Khmer Rouge Cambodia, and elsewhere.

While it is the task of science to discover the new, it is the task of history and literature to explore and express what lies in human experience. Historians and story writers in our time stand before *the great Why?* of the century that separates us from the founding fathers of the secular world. Why did the 20th century just elapsed — putatively liberated from the superstitions of the past by the prophets of the new belief systems — why did the emancipated 20th century not fulfill its sunny forecast? Why was it instead a century that — for all the technological marvels and improvements to daily life — would produce bloody power regimes that carried out genocides against their subjects and victims on an absolutely unprecedented scale? Did something vital to humanity, something fundamental to civilized life, get lost as new religions of man displaced the ancient and traditional faith in the God of beginnings and time?

The stories in this collection dramatize the implications of that insistent *Why?* They examine the habit of men and women who have ceased to believe in God, to believe, as it has been said, not in *nothing*, but in *anything*. To engage the contradictions of the received wisdom of the time is a central task of fiction, but a fiction that is small has little to add to the literature of any age. Whatever merit readers will find in the stories of this collection, they address, like those of my earlier book *Out of the Riven Century*, larger fundamental human concerns. They seek to dramatize the fierce contradictions that assail the modern mind at the turn to the new century in which we are living.

The materialist paradigm put in place by its founders over a century ago is now crumbling — due not only to the baleful Pandora surprises of Marx, Nietzsche and Freud. We are witnessing in our time the crisis and collapse of Darwinian based biology and paleontology and the emergence of a new paradigm of science and human reality no less momentous than the Copernican Revolution and of the Darwinian Revolution itself of almost 150 years ago. From the Big Bang universe of beginnings, empirically observed and measured, to the mathematically impossible conjunction by chance of the cosmic forces that govern matter, to the unbridgeable chasm separating nonorganic matter from the structure of the simplest living cell, to the sudden "Cambrian explosion" in the fossil record of the major body plans of species simultaneously in geological time, to the stubborn nonappearance in that record of transitional forms linking the great divisions of the living world, to the stunning intricacy and complexity of the cells of life—in all these things we are witnessing the demise of the accidental universe and the death of Darwinian chance—the mainspring of a grand, now failed theory. Science itself has revealed that we do not inhabit a universe of chaos and a chance-evolved living world, but a terrestial and cosmic reality that in all its dimensions bears witness to beginning, order, and design.

In the expanding light of science and all knowledge, history's reflection is our trusted guide. History is *all we know*. For science—we must remind ourselves—is part of history too, its past checkered by uncritical premises, failed theories, and displaced certitudes. Let those of critical mind recall earlier enthusiasms for an eternal "steady-state" universe, for the long reign of Haeckel's faked embryo drawings and the fraudulent Piltdown Man, for eugenics, and for the once unassailable theory of a disastrous, man-engendered "global cooling" effect prevalent just a short 20 years ago—lately replaced by an equally unassailable theory of a disastrous, man-caused "global warming."

We have entered a time in history and in the history of science when it is no longer deniable that we live in a world and universe of intricate, almost infinitely complex design and balance. The belief that blind and aimless matter is all there is can no longer be sustained. We have no other choice—by reason and evidence—than humbly to recognize again the Author of beginning and design, the

Creator God who is the motive Spirit of our universe, our world, and our purpose on this planet in historical time.

No civilization can survive severed from its spiritual core. A secularized Western World that does not remember and reawaken to its humanist grounding in the Judeo-Christian revelation that is the very basis of historical time will lack the moral resolve to defeat a powerful, ruthless, suicidalist terrorist enemy in whom humanism has no resonance and who has declared worldwide jihad to destroy the West and subject its men and women to a new and freedomless Dark Age. But if we and our values are but the chance products of a deterministic world without objective morality or ultimate meaning, who are we to claim special civilizational privilege? Why not advise our grandchildren to choose sharia law and survive? These stories dramatize and question the secular creeds that lead inevitably to that relativist mindset, creeds that provide no answer to those questions.

The six stories that follow are about: the strange haunting of a famous Darwinian paleontologist; a Marxist bishop in the late Cold War and his temptation; a modern liberal intellectual standing before the bleak impasse of abandoned faith; a Nietzschean novelist whom honesty compels to confront the great and insistent *Why?* of 20th century disorder and genocide; a Freudian academic surprised by a son's love; and a widely reported revisit to Earth at the end of the 20th century by a famous mysterious stranger from the violent century's beginning.

These stories depict Americans compelled to face unexpected contradictions of the secular, materialist ideas and belief systems now passing that largely formed the world into which they came. Great insistent ironies pervade the national culture in our time. Ironies beg always for attention, and life would be unlivable without humor's saving grace. Attempts to employ both those attributes of serious fiction may be found in what follows.

Nickell John Romjue
Yorktown, Virginia
September 2006

DARWIN'S BLACK BOX

If it could be demonstrated that any complex organ existed which could not possibly have been formed by numerous, successive, slight modifications, my theory would absolutely break down.

— Charles Darwin

I

DENTON HAD NEVER covered a story in which every single element was so shot through with the comic and bizarre. Piloting his brother-in-law's old hearse up the six-lane connector to Diablo, he half expected to feel a clammy hand on his shoulder and turn to see Edgar Allan Poe clambering up from the chamber of last rides to pursue the strange tale beside him. Ahead, a great cloud of blackbirds wheeled in the sky, arrowing westward toward the Front Range, and Denton glanced sidewise at the empty seat just to make sure.

Though the mutual guerrilla raids of Huxel and Vindalin-Nels were standard faculty-fight fare at Diablo, Huxel's clash with Faust, Wolfman of the Rockies, verged on atomic war. The talk-show host's bomb blasts reminded Denton of the fold-out classic of a 'sixties presidential campaign in which the mushrooming hair of the shoot-from-the-hip candidate morphed into a billowing Hiroshima cloud.

Huxel's clashes with Faust and Vindalin-Nels, however, were mere side oddities in the larger weirdness of the Diablo drama. For starters, the great stone face the spring landslides had uncovered above the cliff of Mount Bartlett — a heavy-browed rock form bearing an uncanny resemblance to the famous physiognomy of the Father of Evolution, had set news antennae vibrating all over the country and not just at the supermarket check-outs. Indeed, as the sesquicentennial of *The Origin of Species* approached, it seemed that Nature herself was weighing in to celebrate the material and psychic basis of the modern age. But beyond all comprehension was the stunning publication of the revolutionary claim that Darwin, evolution's Adam and the grandfather of the modern world, had gotten it wrong about the very basis of life, the cell. Seen through the crude optics of 150 years ago, the living cell had been, for Darwin, no more than an amorphous blob of mystery — a "black box".

Adding local insult to the black-box claim was Vindalin-Nels' outrageous painting of it. The portrait rendered by Diablo's eccentric drama arts professor posed the evolutionary father gazing with astonishment into an opened, black, trunk-like box, out of which streamed blinding light.

Add to those bizarre events, the "sightings". Nearly every week since the millennial turn, in Diablo's lecture chambers and hallways, in the faculty club, even in a men's restroom, credible witnesses were reporting the appearance of a small, bearded figure whose features beneath a protruding, "beetling" brow and whose formal black, 19th century dress gave him an unmistakable resemblance to photo images of history's most famous biologist.

Distracted by these bizarre indications, Denton saw suddenly on the dial that the hearse was travelling eighteen miles over the limit along Diablo's notorious speed trap, lucrative courtroom net for woozy returnees from student party-nights in the city. Braking the big unfamiliar vehicle, he felt the hearse swerve, dislodging unknown cargo riding unsecured behind, possibly some of Ike's, his brother-in-law's, military surplus or hunting gear.

But wasn't the rule of the zany and bizarre the norm at Diablo — to be brutally honest, as every reporter ought to be? In fact, his alma mater was almost as unstrung as fabled Berkeley by the Bay. Denton recalled his own graduation day back before the Wall fell, the ceremony registered indelibly in collegiate behavioral history, when a dozen Diablan "streakers for peace" — women as well as men, their private parts imaginatively color-markered red, white, and blue — threw off their robes in a spring cavorting witnessed by thousands.

Darwin's black box, great stone faces, atomic strikes, apparitions, Poe in the hearse — where was the one sane *lead* in the tintintabulation of the bells, bells, bells he was assigned to report and relate coherently to mile-high news consumers in the *Rocky Mountain Sun's* next-week feature-series? He didn't have *one* lead — he was overwhelmed with leads, every one of them zany beyond belief. Long since convinced that shelving Woolf, Plath and deadly text theory for the wired thrill and unending amazements of Fourth Estate life had been life's right decision, Denton knew one thing: the culture wars were alive and well on the Front Range. Spirit invigorated, he gunned up the hearse, eager for the challenge of the day.

II

Faust had a talk-show following you couldn't underestimate, and he kept them charged. The uncanny stoneface of Charles Darwin that Mother Nature had literally unearthed, and which tourist and native eye could spot and identify from the interstate even without binoculars, was simply too good to be true. The radio-man heard by "Faustees" all over the Rockies smelled an evolutionary rat, and he spotlighted his target culprit with relish. It was eight in the morning, and Denton nudged the hearse's radio on-button to catch the latest emotive blast.

Franklin Faust's unhinging of Heinrich Huxel, Darwin apostle and Diablo's paleontologist star, was either a work of art in the AM spectrum or an unconscionably evil neocon jihad, depending on perspective.

Faust's high-pitched voice invaded the aural space of the hearse. "This just in for you Diablo dipsticks! I've got some good ones today for all you moonbeams, so put down your bongs and bongo drums and listen up to what sane Coloradans really think about you snivelling little-boy-beard phonies and retromingent cutesies!"

Denton turned the dial up slightly, pondering whether he might be hearing etymological originals, even breakthroughs, in the mother tongue's lexicon of insult.

"You too, Huxie!" 'Fangs' Faust personally addressed his celebrity enemy. "This is 'Fangs-Boy' calling!" — the radio host working a Diablo return-insult into his routine. "I know you're listening, Huxel. You can't stay away, can you, 'Pink Shades'?"

This was a reference, Denton knew, to the famous paleontologist's unfortunate sun sensitivity, against which he wore a "signature" pith helmet on campus and field expedition year around.

"Just keep that little pithy squashed down on that pinhead of yours," Faust continued his gifted taunt. "And any other of you dipsticks that've just tuned in, listen up to old Fangsie. He's about to howl!"

Edging right in the slow lane as his rear-view mirror caught the flash of what looked like a multicolor car closing in on his bumper, Denton reached too late to cut the volume. Faust's signature wolf-scream sounded through the hearse like a call of Hell. The talk-man's follow-up was hard to hear through the ringing in his ears.

"... *orning* Colorado! Good *Morning*, Nietzsche-land of the Rockies! And how are all my little *uber*-manlets and *uber*-ladies this morning? By the way, I exaggerate about you 'ladies'. And who's *uber* who today? Or should I say *whom* for you ditsy Diablo degenerates?"

Wondering if Faust had ever contemplated a need for a bodyguard or body armor, Denton became suddenly aware of intense scrutiny coming from the small Nissan, covered with bright paint splotches, now passing on his left. As he turned, he saw the car was crammed to the gills with bearded and beaded people. Slowing to let it go by, he immediately recognized his mistake in borrowing Ike's vehicle for the Diablo run. Scarcely four feet away, an ag-

gregate of distorted student physiognomy, male and female, mouthed what were surely obscene epithets in his
direction—which they emphasized with a waving tangle
of fists and high signs thrust out the right-side windows of
the speeding car.

The explanation, of course, was that Ike, named for the
Victor of Normandy, had plastered the back of the hearse
with adhesive exemplars of subtle and crude humor.
Denton recalled seeing, before he'd climbed in, "Imagine
Whirled Peas!" and "Global Warming—Just More Eco-
Crazies' Hot Air!" When he reached Diablo, he'd have to
find a parking garage away from the campus where Ike's
mortality wagon wouldn't receive final death damage—
and then back it in.

The Diablo car pulled ahead down the middle lane,
its own trunk lid and rear bumper revealing a plaster of
sticker provocations and urgent warnings from the opposite side of the spectrum, some scatological. But now, a
bright yellow flash appeared a lane over from the Nissan.
Passing the small vehicle, the big Hummer was trailing
an improbable artillery piece, which looked to Denton's
army-service expertise like a 75-mm. pack howitzer. As he
took in the moving tableau, the Nissan heads—there must
have been six or seven—swivelled to the left as if on cue
to survey the tank-like vehicle, atop which two antlered
carcasses were bound with rope. Through the Hummer's
tinted glass, Denton's eye caught the glint of metal and, as
a window began to open, flashes of hunter-orange outer-
wear.

For years afterward, Denton would regret not holding

out with his editor for a cameraman who could have re-corded what ensued — surely unique in all annals of road rage. News instinct quick, he dropped the driver-side win-dow in order to better witness the ecocratic — gun-rights incident fast shaping up. As he watched, the fist-tangle thrust itself out the left side of the feisty Nissan to menace its new target of outrage. Denton was just processing the hope that the Nissan driver still had one good hand on the wheel, when the Hummer's side window came all the way down and a set of white moons thrust itself into the wind.

Dropping back slightly for less neck strain, while en-deavoring to miss no detail of the road-rage spectacle and hold the road at the same time, Denton saw the flash of the paint gun cylinder just as the glob hit the Hummer mooner, a red explosion that the wind took with it, flaming down the yellow tank's length like a fire-blast and blood-splotching the death-muzzle of the pack howitzer. The hit slowed the hunter vehicle momentarily as the Nissan, its shrieking occupants high-signing with glee, sped away. Only a moment, however, did the hunter wagon hesitate, accelerating to rapidly draw abreast of the fleeing attack sedan.

What followed, Denton grasped instinctively, was the original and first-ever paint-balled, mooner-triggered, dead-raccoon assault in the history of road-rage revenge. As the Hummer bullied into the Nissan's lane, a muscular arm emerged from the right front window of the bloodied tank to fling the ring-tailed corpse of a slaughtered rac-coon dead-on into the Nissan's windshield, smashing it and sending the maimed car across the hearse's path to a quick roadside stop — Denton braking sharply to avoid a collision. Leaving the crippled assailant behind, the hunter panzer exited the carnage scene in a power blast fuelled at its fabled 9-miles to the gallon. Disappearing in the distance, the Hummer, its luckless antlered slaughter riding the roof, hurtled down the connector toward Diablo like a horned Hell-machine.

III

Denton was still half dazed when he pulled into the parking garage three blocks from the campus. Whatever lay ahead in his two-day news mission to capture the Darwin story, he expected that nothing he would see or hear could possibly top the mooner-raccoon assault. Not to short-change the exotic, bizarre and occasionally violent atmosphere he was entering. At Diablo, neither the fall of the Berlin Wall nor 9/11 seemed yet to have significantly registered — though *relevant* concerns had.

Recumbent figures, some sleeping, occupied the sun-warmed brickways leading onto the campus. Denton's eye was immediately taken by an absorbed mentor-pupil team. Reclining alongside an alpenhorn-like wind instrument longer than his own body, a wild-eyed man with a ragged beard blew sepulchral notes through the wooden tube. A young male understudy lay curled up close by, fascinated, taking in technique.

Denton walked on, further recording the Diablo-normal morning. He passed a duelling duo, accordion and guitar, young women whose dancing eyes duelled, too. Will Take Abuse 4 Money, said the hand-printed sign of an artist whose hostile eyes dared Denton to reward his wit. Up the brickway, and everywhere Denton looked, *Self-expression* was the message, art's easy dogma in the enlightened postmodern age, all can play, we are art, inside us are worlds.

Performing from his perch on the low wall of a fountain, a bongo man drummed earnestly, his nine-year-old boy in accompaniement, the show watched impassively by a worn young woman, baby in sling. At the corner, an old man with matted hair foraged in a trash barrel, and at the Che bench, a full-breasted girl with tight overall-shorts and no brassiere nestled for attention by the bronze revolutionary, reading *The Motorcycle Diaries*.

He spotted Vindalin-Nels, wearing a black turtleneck and ponytail, at the agreed rendezvous, which was Vindalin's own bronze sculpture, a great tusked boar that stood out in front of the cavernous old movie theater the artist had converted to use as a combination studio-gallery and practice stage for his student troupe.

Denton liked hogs and was glad Vindalin had suggested the propitious meeting place. His interviewee was rubbing one of the tusks as he came up. Recognizing Denton and with no wasted word of greeting, Vindalin turned on his heel. "Follow me."

Inside, they mounted the stairs to an old, flat-floored balcony widened out at the wings and wrapped semicircularly above the stage below. Stripped of seats and lightened by skylights Vindalin had put in, the artist's studio revealed several portrait paintings, as well as sculptures, human and animal.

There was activity down on the stage, on one side of which Denton observed an easel with a painting. From the distance, he recognized Vindalin's portrait of the bald man sitting by an open treasure chest full of golden light. In the stage center, Vindalin's students were practicing their moves and lines. All of them were wearing tight black outfits of one kind or another and, in bursts of energy, taking theatrical leaps across the wooden boards, which creaked at every impact.

"That's Darwin's black box—*my* version," Vindalin told Denton, pointing down to the easel. "It's the soul of the play, its tocsin. I set it down there to inspire them so they'll keep their minds on the play and not on each other." Moving to the balcony rail, he called down: "Okay, boys and girls. Go through the whole thing. Use the script only if you have to. But keep it down—no shouting and no fooling around! I've got an interview up here, darlings."

"They're a managerie, but I love them," Vindalin said. "They soothe my soul—which needs it."

Denton didn't have to ask why: Huxel. About whom, he hoped, he could draw out the eccentric drama professor-artist. He had long since learned to ask the big questions first, and he did.

"Why did you paint your portrait—Darwin and the 'black box'? And what made you write a play about it?" Denton sat down to take notes. No recording, no cameraphone, nothing electronic, Vindalin had said.

"I'll tell you why," the artist replied, continuing to

walk around while throwing an occasional glance down at the energy display below. "When an intriguing idea comes my way, I try to paint it—or shape it, sculpt it. That's how I can *understand* it. I look for the *visual meaning* of the image. The meaning of the black box is pretty significant. When I realized that, I thought—why not give my students something big to chew on? Why not *stage* Darwin and his black box too?"

"That book about it must be pretty powerful." Denton interrupted.

"Indeed it is. I was in a bookstore one day, just browsing. They had just gotten in the paperback of this intriguing title I'd heard about, *Darwin's Black Box*. I picked it up. It was about what Charles Darwin didn't and couldn't know about biochemistry in 1859 and what microbiologists know today. I thought, hmm, this could be startling. I bought it."

"By the way," Vindalin added. "Just when I picked up my copy, Huxel came in the bookstore. He was angry. He went right to the display and grabbed up the whole stack—every one—bought 'em all, and went out."

"Why did Professor Huxel do that?"

Vindalin smiled. "Why did the ancient Egyptian priests screen off the temple secrets?"

"I'm no scientist," Vindalin went on. "But I've got a mind. Darwin had only the faintest dream of the interior of a cell, not to speak of how it worked. For him, it *was* a black box. And he theorized that, when something reproduced, cells just "naturally", randomly, by chance, mutated—*evolved*. That's the basic idea of *The Origin of Species*

— that *random* mutations evolved life through the simple organic structures in every living thing that he thought cells actually were. That's all he could get out of the optics of the 1850s. Then along came Watson and Crick and DNA in our time and opened up the whole question, unlocked the secrets of the cell."

"Anyway, I was struck by this image: Just what emotion would register in Darwin's face if he could return to earth now — when his successors have opened the black box? I wanted to paint the face of Darwin as he lifted the lid."

"So that's what I did, and I'll show it to you in a minute if they don't knock it down first." Vindalin stopped pacing and moved quickly to the balcony rail. "Hey! Break it up down there!" he shouted. Turning, Denton looked over the rail to see a pas-de-deux pair in close arrested motion, entwined and kissing deeply.

"So then I wrote my play — one act — that's all *this* blockbuster needed. It's their semester project. But then one of them wanted to photograph the painting, and I let him. He gave it to the student newspaper, *The Breeze*. That's when the s — hit the fan."

"I imagine Professor Huxel was surprised," Denton said.

"Huxel went ballistic. He called me up and asked me what a two-bit artist and theater instructor knew about science. Then he said it was too bad Hitler didn't get *all* my family. But then he took that back and apologized — after a fashion. I 'didn't know s — ,' he told me. As I say, it *did* hit the fan. I told him, number one, he should visit Auschwitz some time, and number two, he should read the book he's afraid of. Then I cut him off, the son-of-a-bitch! Wait till he hears about the play."

Vindalin paced the gallery again, cooling off.

"How do your students like the play?" Denton asked.

"They tell me it's 'cool'. I put Mrs. Darwin in it, too. Not the real Mrs. Darwin, you understand, but a young wife who makes Darwin's life interesting. It's a comedy — doesn't it have to be? You should see the wife's costumes they've come up with—imaginative to say the least! I can't always keep my wild little troupe under control—as you've just seen."

"Anyhow, the fossils man will turn blue when we stage 'The Last Days of Darwin'," Vindalin finished off. "Now let's go down and look at *my* take on *Darwin's Black Box.*"

In the portrait image of the great biologist who had rocked the firmament of the world almost 150 years ago — his bright gaze beneath the famous rounded brow familiar to generations the world over — Darwin sat on a high stool staring intensely into the black, treasure-chest-like container on the stand before him.

Blinding, white-gold light streamed up from the open lid. Against the brightness, the figure had raised one hand as if to shield his eyes. But into the riveted gaze of Darwin, the artist had painted an expression of profound shock. The blinding stream of light from the black box was new light. Was the light revelation?

"Huxel *hates, hates, hates* my *Darwin*," Vindalin said. "I'm told he went from blue to purple when he saw the photo. But did I tell you? He then sent a stooge to try to *buy* my painting—for five-hundred dollars! I was too smart. Don't ever sell your painting to somebody it's made mad. The world will never see it again. You know what happened to that painting of Winston Churchill, don't you? The one where he had no feet and looked simian? It disappeared, and nobody can find it."

Denton had read somewhere about the vanished official portrait of the great prime minister. Lady Churchill was the lead suspect.

Now, Denton looked closely at the black-box portrait. In the detail of the widening light-fan streaming out of the opened treasure chest of life, Vindalin had painted, in golden suggestion, the delicate tracery of machine-like structures, conduits, and gateways of the biochemical organism that was the simplest life cell. Fascinated, Denton drew closer to the schematic light-complex.

"Why are you intrigued, and Huxel isn't?" the artist, watching him, said suddenly. "I'm only an artist, not a scientist. Shouldn't scientists want black boxes opened? What is he afraid of?"

"Losing his whole life's work, maybe." Denton said.

"I don't know about that," Vindalin said. "I just paint what reveals itself."

IV

Denton's editor had given him two days to develop the story that he was beginning to believe was not a story at all but a carnival parade of mystery figures and costumed things, an antic assemblage of the real and unreal at the

center of which paced, in uneasy step, the paradoxical figure of Heinrich Huxel. Denton decided that, preparatory
to his scheduled afternoon interview with the celebrity
paleontologist, he would sit in on Huxel's morning lecture class to get a first-hand impression of the best-selling
author of *Rooster's Combs and Donkey's Brays.*

Arriving early, he took a seat high in the steep bank
of desks of the lecture chamber, an autopsy lab of one-
hundred years ago whose low, centered dias— original-
ly placed for the dissection of corpses—now mounted a
lectern. Students streamed in through the ground-level
doors left and right, propped open to the fall air. They
hurried past Huxel's dias to climb to their perches, all of
which soon were taken, the latecomers finding seats in the
banked aisles.

Huxel burst into the autopsy theater like a wind, the
wool-lined mackinaw he wore year-round, open and
lifted by the bustle of his entry. Field-trip ready, he wore
heavy jeans and rugged buff boots and a lumberjack's red-
plaid shirt overlaid with suspenders bearing Indian eagles
and arrowed designs. Pith headgear removed, Huxel had
gray-streaked hair, Native American braided and long,
and a short, trimmed beard, almost white. Slamming a
clipboard of notes down on the lectern, he launched into
his lecture at once, paying no attention to the final trick-
ling in of auditors.

All around Denton, students scribbled assiduously.
Here and there, some, bored and laid-back, eyes wandering, captured the professor's fast clip electronically,
freeing up their minds to analyze details of opposite-sex

ambience. Distracted himself, Denton wondered if any of
the girl students around him would qualify as Faust's female dipsticks. Watching for professorial tics while trying
to follow Huxel's exposition of the Cambrian Explosion
and punctuated equilibrium, he was just lapsing back to
the memory of the flung raccoon, when suddenly a dark
figure on a bicycle hurtled through the right-side door
into the autopsy chamber. All heads swung to follow the
bicycling ape who, reaching the podium, chattered out a
high-pitched scream at the stunned paleontology lecturer
before disappearing out the left-side doorway.

Huxel reacted vigorously and fast, jumping to the
chamber floor. In a fast overarm, he flung his clipboard
after the prankster, sending it sailing out the open door,
notes flying. Following it, Huxel dashed out, shouting as
he pursued the vandal ape, "Stop that Jesus-Land son-of-
a-bitch!"

"Jesus-Land?" This *was* the culture wars.

"Huxel's had it," a student next to Denton exclaimed.
"His nerves are really shot. The 'sightings' and the painting, and now an ape guy harassing him."

"Proffie needin' chillin', " another voice said.

"What about the sightings?" Denton asked. "Who's
doing all this? And have *you* ever seen it—Darwin's
ghost?"

"No, but I know the guy in the ape suit. It's Mueller.
He's one of Vindalin's actors," the student said.

"Maybe your bud Mueller or one of his acting buddies
is playing Darwin's ghost, too?"

"No," the student told Denton. "Mueller's weird,

and he says they're all weird over there. They go around the campus dressed up like Oscar Wilde or Edgar Allan Poe—even Dracula. But they don't know either who the f—Excuse me, Sir. They don't know who the Darwin guy is either."

V

At the campus cafeteria, Denton grabbed a copy of the student newspaper and ordered a big-mouth bacon powerburger and a cinnamon bun—a million calories, but he needed all the energizers he could get in this vortex of vim, vigor and perplexity that more and more was taking on the character and setting of a story it would take a Poe to write.

MOUNT DARWIN was the headline of the lead student editorial. Denton jerked the page close, the powerburger kicking in.

"Why is 'Mount Darwin'—as the powers-that-be are about to name the rock-pile miracle out at Mount Bartlett—why is it *so nicely landscaped* ?" the editorial wondered. "Does Mother Nature use chisels and hoes, bushwhackers?— ever surprising us with Her natural handiwork?"

"You can get to Old Stone Face, which Nature has so mysteriously unveiled, by trail if you've got a couple of hours—which *The Breeze* recently did. Everything around Old Baldy was very . . . *neat*. The underbrush actually looked trimmed. Stoney's beetle brow looked quite amazingly 'natural'. He looked almost . . . *chiselled* !

"Question: Why did they pay good money to the sculptor of Mount Rushmore when Mother Nature, who is the world's acknowledged Greatest Artist, now does her own faces? Or not. Put on your hiking boots and your pith helmet — if you need one — and go see for yourself.

"We report, you decide."

Denton went into a choking fit on his big-mouth bite. He recovered just as a burly student approached, elbows out, ready to administer the Heimlich maneuver. "You all right, Sir?"

"Yaach . . . ack . . . yah!" Denton coughed out. "Thanks, thanks."

Cutting short preparations for the Huxel interview, Denton went straight to the offices of *The Breeze*, his own launching pad twenty short-long years ago, hoping to find the incendiary writer. He was in luck.

"I'm Andy Jackson," the tall, red-haired boy said.

"That is a great name." Denton admired the scrappy president who yielded no ground to any of his offended elite betters. "Your editorial must have been hot to the touch for one of your faculty readers."

"Yes, I've already heard from Professor Huxel." Andy grinned. "He said in his e-mail he wanted to 'unman' me — though he said it a little differently than that."

"Were you serious about the stone face?" Denton asked. "Did it really look like nature had some help?"

"Well, it's not exactly a Rushmore likeness, I guess," the student editor said. "It could be a kind of freak of nature, part of it anyway — he's got quite a granite dome — and brow. And New Hampshire does have *its* 'Great Stone Face'. But some of it looked pretty chipped away on.

But then there weren't any chips—no rubble. Everything looked washed clean . . . *tended*. And the landslide was just last spring."

"What about the 'sightings'?" Denton asked. "Do you think it's Vindalin-Nels' drama students? I hear they get a kick out of impersonating famous people."

"No, I don't think it's them," Andy said. "The sightings are just too strange. We've reported five of them. I make my reporters track down every detail. But it's always the same."

"What do you mean?"

"He *looks* like that photograph of Darwin you see in the books. I've never seen the little man myself. But everybody who has, that we've interviewed, says the same thing. He looks like his picture . . . and he always looks . . . *distraught*.

"And it's always evening or at night, or in some private place. He simply vanishes away. A custodian saw him in the stacks one night, in the library. He was reading a book. The strangest sighting we've reported was in the chancellor's office . . . the receptionist—working late."

"Clammy hand?" Denton smiled.

"Yes!" Andy said. "I interviewed her myself. The hand on her shoulder was real—it was like ice. He was staring at her computer screen."

"That alone must have disturbed him."

"No doubt."

"Maybe people see what they're psyched-up to see."

"Maybe," Andy answered. "But this is a bigger story than sightings and an icy hand and whether Vindalin-Nels would or could pull off a doppelganger stunt to get back at Huxel."

"What do you mean by bigger?" Denton asked again.

"Darwin's 'black box' isn't just Vindalin's amazing painting," Andy replied. "It's the book the microbiologist wrote, and all the other books that have come out about 'the theory in crisis'."

"Darwin was myopic," the student editor said. "Though it really wasn't his fault. It was his optics' 'fault'. He couldn't begin to see into the cell. It *was* a black box. Darwin theorized at the level *above* the cell. So . . . about the cell and the basic structure and chemistry of life, he just guessed. But guess what? In the late twentieth century, along came some amazing technologies like electron microscopy and nuclear magnetic resonance. The result? Darwin's whole theory fails at the molecular level."

"Sorry, you'll have to explain that to me."

"Okay," Andy said, Denton listening, fascinated, to his 21-year-old mentor. "Here it is: Cellular life is based on organic machines, machines that are made of molecules. Fantastic molecular machines operate inside the cell that Darwin couldn't even look into. The machines haul chemical 'cargo' along infinitesimal 'highways'. They operate biochemical 'switches'. They capture energy, allowing electric current to flow. They build other machines that, for example, ingest food. Random mutations—natural selection—just can't explain building amazingly complex machines."

"A colossal *mis*-guess then," Denton said.

"Yes. But how could he have known that something

so infinitesimal, something you can only see as a blob through an 1850s microscope, was so complex? As that book that you can't get a copy of around here, says — think of a watch . . . a tiny cog gets bent ever so slightly, and the watch stops. It doesn't 'evolve' to a better watch."

"But watches do improve," Denton said. "Watches can evolve."

"Yes, but it takes a watchmaker to 'evolve' them. Evolve is a murky word, isn't it? A watchmaker doesn't evolve anything, he designs, redesigns it. Chance isn't in his working vocabulary. If it were, his watches wouldn't run."

"You can't get around it," Andy went on. " 'Chance' isn't very scientific. Darwin was only guessing about the black box he couldn't see into. But now, we know. Except his successors won't let go of the grand 19th-century idea that supposedly made everything so simple. The big problem is, Darwinian evolution is holy scripture. Darwin's a holy of holies it's anathema to disturb. It's like Lenin's Tomb. Marx is history and Lenin is dead, but the corpse lives on. The truth is," Andy finished off his irreverent critique, "Darwinism is less a scientific theory than an a priori philosophical principle. It's the philosophy that counts, not the facts."

"But aren't you just going back to 'creationism' when you say 'design'? God created everything eight or ten thousand years ago including the Grand Canyon as is, along with all the fossils in the rocks?"

"Of course not. That's just the way the Darwinian Schoolmen try to marginalize the evidence of design. They deliberately. . .they disingenuously conflate some people's belief in young-earth creationism, which they don't fear, with the Big Bang universe and ancient earth and record of life that, in every known particular, demonstrate order and design. *That*, they do fear. You need to read the book."

"Well!" Denton said. "I don't know whether Darwin is on the way out or not, but *you've* got a future, I think."

"I hope so, if I can only get out of here with a degree. Diablo's professors aren't all captains of courage. A lot of people are intimidated by Huxel—and by Darwin. They'd rather sweep Darwin's guess under the rug, keep the implication of the black box black . . . they might be ridiculed, lose their grants." Andy shrugged.

"I think I understand why Huxel is rattled, and not just about apparitions," Denton said.

"It collapses his world," Andy said.

"You must be a biology major."

"No . . . though it's my minor. But you don't even have to be a biology minor to get all this. You just have to be able to read what the biologists, the biochemists who've opened the black box say."

"It does sound revolutionary," Denton said.

"It is. The unlocking of the cell is one of the greatest achievements in the history of science. This is *scientific* stuff, *empirical* stuff. These are facts, they're not guesses. This isn't the science that papers over missing links—transitional forms that keep evading all attempts to find them going on 150 years."

"You do your homework, don't you?"

"Well, isn't that what we're supposed to do, instead of just swallowing the received wisdom?"

"We're supposed to," Denton answered. "But there are some unwritten codes out there that say: 'keep swallowing'."

"Like what?"

"You already know. Like questioning the holy of holies. Like Marx, and maybe Darwin."

"Marxism is dead."

"It is now. But it wasn't dead where I work or at the TV anchor desks, till the Wall came down and the Soviet Union imploded. You're too young to remember. You should have seen and read the uproar when Ronald Reagan said 'Tear down this wall!' They called him a warmonger, a right-wing fanatic—a *19th-century throwback*. Hmm, how's that for irony?"

"I've read about it, of course. But why were they like that?"

"Why?" Denton said. "Politically correct, peer pressure, knowing that your anchor or editor will get mad and sideline you. But most of all, we went easy on the socialist dream because we didn't think for ourselves. We even tried to bury Solzhenitsyn when we found out he wasn't just anti-Stalin, he was anti-socialism all the way! Maybe it's the same with neo-Darwinism today. You get ridiculed and sidelined, shouted down."

"Well, I won't get shouted down" Andy said, waving at a print of Old Hickory pinned up on the wall behind him. "I've got my hero. Anyway, what does a 'critical approach' to the news or to anything mean when it's so selective and not 360 degrees all around? If they think they can bury the black box or smother the Cambrian Explosion — thousands of new species all at once in geological time — or ignore the uncanny tolerances of the Big Bang universe and the chemistry of the earth — they've already lost. I can't wait to get out of here. I'll start my own magazine if I have to, my own blog, too."

"If I were my editor, I'd hire you today," Denton said.

"Keep me in mind," Andy smiled. "Here, take this," he said, handing Denton a book. "It's the 'incendiary' that has really set things off. But I need it back when you leave. Huxel's goons keep cleaning out the bookstores."

"Some ideas around Diablo U. sound too hot to handle," Denton responded.

"Read all about it on the internet," Andy laughed. "The genie's out of the bottle."

VI

Huxel had postponed the afternoon interview, Denton found out when he showed up at the department. "He will see you, but just for a few minutes, tomorrow morning at eight," the secretary said.

Denton decided he'd use the time to take a look at Mount Darwin in advance of tomorrow's ceremony — the final piece of his story. Climbing the interstate's long ascent to the pass, beyond which lay the natural apparition in stone, he had the sensation of a 'sighting' of his own — maybe a new variety in the Fourth Estate's own species. Denton mulled over the network fiasco of a partisan producer-anchor team who had boldly exploited forged documents to try to bias an election result. He meditated on a future of young journalists without gates to confine them, unafraid of anyone or anything, not even of the modern-postmodern zeitgeist whose underpinings were crumbling. No wonder Diablo had a restless ghost.

From the elaborate new tourist turnout on the interstate, Denton judged the crow-fly distance to the rock physiognomy above the mountain cliff at a half-mile at least. The reports weren't too exaggerated. The fascinating visage brought to light by nature's rains had a more than fair resemblance to the great icon. Through his binoculars, Denton observed a bald dome and beetling brow overhanging deep eye sockets: the new natural wonder looked almost as real through the glasses close-up as from afar. Small wonder that Huxel's campaign for Mount Darwin had succeeded. "It's nature's Mount Rushmore," Denton recalled his own paper's Huxel quotation, cited soon after the landslide news. " 'Mount Darwin' will attract tourists by the tens of thousands," the Diablo celebrity had added for legislative ears.

Standing beside Denton at the lookout, a small boy gazed at the distant stone. "Who's that bald old man?" he chirped back to his family, who were just piling out of a van with California plates and about to confirm the result of Huxel's sly legislative pitch. "I don't know," his little sister said, coming up to look. "Whoever it is, he sure looks unhappy."

VII

At the hotel, Denton opened the book Andy had given him, the bound document that was Huxel's horror and the inspiration of Vindalin-Nels. The biologist's book was forceful and methodical — amazing stuff! Where had a scientist learned to write clear English prose? In fact it was midnight before Denton put the book down.

Rolling out of bed the next morning, he felt drugged . . . dragooned by the dream, as if he had been dragged bodily somehow into this strangest of all the stories he had ever covered. Even *Poe* had gotten into it! Poe, whose cadences since seventh grade he'd been unable to get out of his mind — had muscled his way in. What could Poe have known about Darwin? Was it the *black box* that had activated the sepulcher seeking genius of the weird and bizarre? Evolution might have serious problems indeed, but neurological science had whole labyrinths to explore in the 21st century — maybe starting with him — Denton! Chugging his coffee, he wondered if he had stepped inadvertently into an old armoire and was now actually resident in some new Narnia-land. Or maybe this week the whole human race had taken an evolutionary leap forward — or backward.

The dream exchange was vivid, crazy and amazing, and Denton wondered if he ought to write it down. No, better keep sources/ghosts/dreams segregated here — if that was any longer possible. Poe's questions to the Father of Evolution had lacked all tact, and he hadn't gone easy on Huxel either, with Andy and Vindalin-Nels and a disembodied Faust all chiming in. *The Raven* poet's feisty directness, which his New England critic-ghosts, twirling in their graves, were still smarting from, came out strongly.

"I have sent for thee, holy friar," Poe addressed Darwin. "I would not call thee fool, old man . . .

But you are the *finch man*, I hear —
(The affair seems pale and drear).
Tell me now about the finches,
And the droughts as they have lifted,
And the beaks the seeds have sifted,
Yet returned to what they were of yore,
Beaks renewed no longer, nevermore.

"You are an ignoramus and a known drunk!" Huxel had shot out.

"I do not know who *you* are, Sir, but I readily see that you are an ass!" Poe returned hotly.

"*Yes, he is!!*" Vindalin affirmed, ponytail bouncing.

"No." Denton's 21-year-old friend Andy now broke into the fantastic dream exchange. "Our professor-star is actually a new species of Luddite. He has a problem with machines — cells' biochemical machines that are so intricate and complex that if Mr. Darwin's random mutations alter them, close just one of their little biochemical switches, the cells don't 'evolve', they crash."

"But that would destroy the whole theory!" Darwin was aghast. "If any complex organ cannot possibly have been formed by numerous, successive changes in its cells, my theory has broken down! A species could not evolve into another species!"

"You got it, Charlie baby!" Faust's tenor zinged in. "You're an honest old coot. Unlike Starch-Butt over there. What do you say now, Fossil Man, you unmitigated fraud? Fossils everywhere but none of them connected. No precious 'transitional forms' after all, you dumb bastard. And you heard it from the big cahuna himself, the original horse's mouth!"

"No 'primordial soup' miracle, either, no spontaneous life from lightning," Vindalin weighed in. "Huxel knows all about *that* experiment that they quietly shelved — they found out the early-earth chemistry was all wrong — but he teaches it anyway."

"It was? He does?" Darwin exclaimed.

"But . . . but, the Theory! *The Theory has primacy!*" Huxel shouted. "Material factors we haven't discovered yet! Future biologists will find them!"

"I see," Poe commented meditatively. "Evolution *has to* be true. But is it then not science truly, but *belief* . . . and *un-rule-y?*"

"Haven't you had all of 140 years — plus," Andy replied to Huxel. "Face it. The esteemed gentleman's theory fails with the cell itself — fails at the basic, molecular level. That's the action arena! It's over with! The emperor has no clothes."

"I don't?" Darwin said, looking, puzzled, at his own naked form, whose undress Denton now noticed for the first time.

"And you're next, Starch-Butt!" Faust shouted. "Strip off, Huxie, and start running. Streakers for dead creeds!"

"How shall the burial rite be read? The solemn song be sung?" the poet recited.

"What remains is this," Denton's nominee for the reform of American journalism continued cooly: "Design. Design isn't just apparent. It's manifestly evident wherever you look, microcosm and cosmos — intricacy beyond all imagination. It's a no brainer. What was Occam's Razor?" he continued. "It was that the simplest rational explanation of any complex thing carries the day. Aimless, random selection, chance mutations, a theory resting on a purposeless jumble of billions of mathematically impossible little miracles of chance. Who's credulous here anyway? It's like the earth-centered heavens and the planets jitterbugging back and forth in orbit before Galileo came along with his optics. But now we have *super-* optics."

"It's not your father's microcosm," Andy finished off, glancing slyly at Huxel.

"I did not have those. . .'supers'," Darwin said, shaking his head.

"Not your fault, Sir," Andy responded.

"It's Starch-Butt's fault!" Faust shot out again. "You're history, Huxie. Next stop for Pink Shades? Ret-set condo in South Beach and your own balcony lab . . . cleavage telescopy!"

"Florida is 'red state,'" Vindalin commented. "He wouldn't be happy."

"Over many a quaint and curious volume of forgotten lore," Poe was saying as the dream began to fade. . .which was probably a good thing. Denton's head was swimming in spite of the third cup of hotel gourmet blend, which he could barely drink. Irreducibly complex sets of intricate, interdependent, calibrated, *effectively unalterable* biochemical machines?

Denton looked out the westward window of his room at the dramatic upthrust of the Rockies escarpment, the sunrise moving down its steep wall. He recalled a history lecture he had heard at Diablo twenty years ago about the waning of the Scholastic Age and the opening of the world. Was his own age like that distant time at the dawn of the New Learning when an intellectual thrombosis paralyzed the stagnant academies of Europe, their avatars in adamant resistance, furious before the new light, zealous to quiet the heretic Copernicus, suppress the revolutionary question of the age?

VIII

Huxel's office, palatial in size, was crowded with artifacts, souvenirs and framed photographs from the paleontologist's expeditions. Denton had never seen so many bones outside museum rooms, or in the burial cave he had once seen at Oppenheim on the Rhine, an ossuary of the anonymous mass dead of the Thirty Years War.

There were labelled specimens everywhere, each case and table fastidiously neat. Behind Huxel's polished great desk, neatly appointed with treasures of the hunt — a tooth in amber, a "humanoid" skull — hung an oil portrait that Denton guessed was a commissioned replica. Glancing up

at the Father of Evolution, Denton involuntarily smiled —
Vindalin's incendiary image flashing through his mind.

"What's funny?" Huxel, watching him closely, shot out
verbally from behind the desk. Facing Denton across the
polished surface, his hefty interviewee looked like a lord of
the castle. Standing like an underling before him, Denton
was startled momentarily by the image of *two* Huxels —
the scientist's torso doppelganger stretching menacingly
toward him across the shiny plane. Recovering quickly
and setting his smile, Denton said: "I'm the friendly face
of the *Rocky Mountain Sun*. And thanks for letting me interview you."

"Five minutes, maybe ten," Huxel said, not getting up.
"Take a seat. What does the Rocky Mountain Sun think it
needs to know?"

Denton sat down. Watching him, Huxel had begun to
judo-chop the desk with his right hand in a steady, slow
repetition, his eye fixed on Denton like a D.A. Was he
dreaming again? Slightly unnerved and certain of a vola-
tile interview anyway, Denton discarded his lead-ups and
asked the pointed question.

"How do you explain the book about the 'black
box'?"

"That son-of-a-bitch!" Huxel shouted. "I've got to stop
him!" But, suddenly glancing at his watch, he swivelled
his chair, reached and punched the button of the radio behind him.

Faust's high-tenor taunt invaded the paleontology
chamber. "We've checked you out, Pinhead. Your 'Mount
Darwin' is a colossal fraud. And guess what, Squirrelly —

you devious little devil that likes to take mountain hikes with a mallet and a chisel . . . ."

Huxel's face flashed red. To Denton, the paleontologist's whole ample body seemed to swell up, the effect doubled by the mirror of the desk.

"No wonder 'Old Stone Face' looks so pretty and clean." Faust continued. "Rodin himself couldn't have done better."

"What?! What?!" Huxel jumped in his chair. "You redneck bastard! You cretin!"

". . . Now listen up, Huxie. Mother Nature may have a little surprise for you when old 'Guv-Guv' does his little dedication this p.m. So keep your beady little eyes on 'Old Baldy'."

Denton watched in alarm as Huxel overturned the swivel chair, lunging to grab a large bone — a femur? — from his desk. Smashing it down on the plastic case of the radio, he silenced his tormenter, the blow also shattering the bone specimen.

"Get out, get out!" Huxel shouted at Denton.

Denton grabbed his equipment and moved to the door. But just as he turned to glance back, the room abruptly quieted. Professor Huxel was standing, unmoving, a dozen feet back from the long casement windows of his office, which looked out on a small shaded courtyard. Following his gaze, Denton saw the small figure, framed full length in the glass. He was wearing an old-fashioned, close-fitting black suit with a vest. His eyes, beneath the heavy brow, burned intensely, staring into the interior of the room. Darwin's apparition, doppelganger in time, gifted understudy of Vindalin-Nels — whoever the strange figure was that Denton was now beholding — stared fixedly past the trophy cases and table displays directly at his Diablo disciple. Huxel was screaming as he lifted the smashed radio and with both hands hurled it at the window, the shattered glass falling in angry shards as the figure disappeared into the shrubbery of the courtyard.

IX

Pulling into the lookout, Denton parked the hearse where the cop pointed. The parking lot was almost full, the television crews and Diablo officials mixing with the governor's party. They had set up a long table, with champagne and coffee and a lavish buffet. At the table, two obese students gorged boldly under the disapproving eye of the chancellor. Though he had witnessed Huxel's final nudge-to-the-edge, Denton was still surprised at the professor's no-show.

In the distance, Darwin looked down with satisfaction upon the dedication party. As Denton surveyed the Rushmore of the Rockies, as he now heard a TV reporter chattering the phrase out to unseen thousands, he wondered about the mallet-and-chisel theories. In the clear light that nature had scripted for dedication day, the resemblance was eery and undeniable.

The governor, a lean rancher type who Denton knew was actually an electronics entrepreneur, had just launched his remarks when suddenly, before all eyes, the crime of Taliban proportion occurred — an ultimate vandal

act after which there was nothing left to say. A brownish
dust cloud enveloped the distant face of Darwin, followed
just one second later by an explosive retort out of the canyon below. In the noise of the shouting and small screams
around him, Denton watched the rubbled cloud fall heavily down the cliff face. Darwin was gone.

———

Cable and network TV reported the destruction of the
stone apparition first, but Denton, writing through the
night, was first with the full award-winning story. Court
processes lay ahead for Franklin Faust and his artilleryized
Second Amendment confederacy. The Faustees, slowed
by their trundled Taliban destroyer and otherwise easy to
spot in a yellow, red-splotched Hummer, were winding
up out of the canyon when the state troopers nailed them,
the pack howitzer's muzzle still hot from the vandalizing
fire.

Taking his ultimate blow from the vivid six p.m. pix-
els, Diablo's paleontology star — later taken into custody
and quieted only by straitjacket — faced charges of assault
by Neanderthal leg bone on the person of Vindalin-Nels,
a crime witnessed in his gallery by Vindalin's whole costumed troupe. Huxel's retirement to the coastal mountains
of Big Sur would follow, where, in the forested fastnesses
of peace, therapies of Eastern persuasion are tendered and
sometimes help.

Vindalin's portrait made the cover of a news magazine,
a first major statement in the national media of the theory
in crisis. Awards under his belt, Denton moved on to a city

of cities where the bizarre is never new but a constant in the dawn of a new time in which the gates of information are gone and the fora are free and the secret of Darwin's black box illuminates the discourse of the world.

THE RED PRIEST AND THE ACTRESS

Liberalism was inevitably pushed aside
by radicalism, radicalism had to surrender
to socialism, and socialism could not stand up
to communism. [Soviet communism] could
endure and grow due to the enthusiastic support
from an enormous number
of Western intellectuals . . . .

— *Aleksandr Solzhenitsyn*

I

DEGLER PAUSED ON the wide stone flight to view the spot where, in a scene even worse in the book than the movie version, the demon-possessed priest came flying through the window to his death on the slabs below. When he'd jogged to the stage Oscar night, Shannon handed all credit to "the Brothers, who taught me to write." Degler had read the book on a flight to the West Coast and wished the Brothers had exorcised Shannon's writing demon in its infancy.

He finished the climb up from the river and came out on a street just below the spires of the university. At some distance beyond, the great ship of the cathedral rose over the city, its towers, in good medieval tradition, still unfinished. Degler's eye dropped abruptly from the Age of Faith to the line of secular facades before him, elegant Georgian townhouse rows whose prices paled the cheeks of newcomers and sent realtors' hearts leaping.

Shannon had built his city-villa on the very setting of "Demons." Here, in that vivid imagination, had occurred the memorable head-spinning scene that made the national flesh crawl. Apparently, Shannon could not leave his inspiration point. He had memoralized it, and his new riches, in a fabled example of Hollywood East secluded behind the Georgian brick. The movie plunder had funded a five story palace, all glass on the river side, with a spectacular circular stair ascending the entire glass face from wine cellar bars to hideaway studio lofts in high half-stories. He had turned one whole floor into a Versailles-like hall of mirrors, all silver and white.

Turning with some curiosity into Shannon's entrance, Degler stopped to examine the regal looking brass plate. Etched within fleur-de-lis borders, just above Shannon's name, was an Oscar statuette.

The gleam of the plate on the adjoining house caught Degler's eye, and he stepped back to read who Shannon's neighbors were:

Technical Creations

He speculated on this oxymoron as he ascended one of a shining white pair of step-cascades to Shannon's door. A metal sculptor with a patron in National Arts? Computer consultants with Georgetown pretensions? A node of some West Coast internet city perhaps, a tony townhouse for visiting Silicon tycoons?

Degler saw at a glance that Shannon's own brass boast was no idle chatter: the place was the ultimate fundraiser. The Give Peace a Chance crowd could not have chosen a better stage, here in the city where the coffers opened widest — to the proper credentials. As soon as the coin in the coffer rings, the vote from "undecided" swings.

A horde of painters and decorators were carrying out

the final whims and touches of Shannon's stage sense. The mirrored hall had an eighteen foot ceiling at least, and from it hung giant new chandeliers. Scrambling along the scaffolding, electricians and carpenters were fitting cables under the white and silver moldings. Degler caught the momentary glint of lenses high in the decorative detail around the tall mirror frames. Did they project? Or did they "watch"? Some of each, probably, in this silvery orgy of Hollywood high tech in the city of no secrets. Clearly, it was going to be a well-staged affair. But leave the *show* to "the Starlet."

Degler made a face at himself in one of the mirrors, the scowl reflecting from the mirror opposite and back, and then to all infinity. To such hands as Mavis Dawn's were entrusted History. Degler was staggered repeatedly by the bizarre whimsy of the dialectic.

The Starlet had not the slightest rational grasp of "new epochs" — not to speak of old ones. No more grasp, in fact, than she had of "nukes."

Nukes, for Mavis, comprehended power plants and billowing Hiroshimas without distinction. It was by their very argument for "peaceful use," Mavis told the rock rallies, that the Generals slipped ever deadlier weapons of doom by us and into production. The whole insane policy was pushing the socialist world, in its desperation to match the New Cold War challenge, to build up their own navy, army, air force, and ICBM's rather than to raise their standard of living as they really wanted to do.

Whenever Degler pondered the brainless non sequiturs of the Starlet's strategic sense, he sank into the slough of despond. Organizing for the antics of the Hollywood crowd might pay the bills between elections, but it didn't do anything for Degler's faith in History—which he took pains to set apart from Mavis Dawn's distinctionless embrace of anyone wearing a red star.

She actually took her "big ideas," she said—and this was on the record—"mainly from films." Two celluloid classics particularly had informed her thinking. These were: "The Russians Are Coming! The Russians Are Coming!" and "Hiroshima, mon Amour."

Degler wondered how far into infinity he was scowling. He was reminded of one of those *New Yorker* cartoons where the barber, looking into the mirrors, sees his client appear as a hairy fiend fore and aft at the fourth reflection. If you had the eyesight of an eagle, say, or of one of those condors wheeling over the California coast ranges, you could, Degler thought, probably see twice as many images of yourself. He strained his eyes to follow his shrinking reflection till it vanished into points of black.

Around him, the decorators chattered. The electricians and the communications men called to one another. Somewhere high in the wall behind him, Degler heard the boring and scratching of others of their kind unseen. He looked again into the mirrors, following the unsmiling images that receded into the endless breadth of the room. As he viewed the mocking depths and the watching clones, he could not put right a sense of time. Image, all action in the mirrored room, evoked only its idiot reflection, arresting the forward press of things, blocking the future as the past lengthened its inexorable span.

For Degler, the past was errant, God-ridden and dead. To the challenges of the Sixties, it had had nothing to say, its New Deals and best new dawns compromised and flawed fatally by its moribund institutions and ebbing faiths. For him there had come a year when all history seemed a vast mockery, a catechistic dream seen through bourgeois trick-lenses, and on the eve of his orals, he had walked out and into the Politics of Change. Don't trust anyone over thirty, they'd said to each other. History begins with 1917, with the Sealed Train — to the Finland Station. And when it was clear that the Change would not come quickly, he joined those who would work from within for equality and for a final justice.

But he was no longer so certain that what he had hoped would lie beyond the false turns and sacrifices of history's great experiment was what man ought to be. He tried to say that his hesitations were only the beguiling irrationalities of the past, but he did not succeed when he tried to do this. The more he beheld of the complex diversity and individuality of life, the less he was able to place the pour of his experience at the end of some mechanistic chain forged over vast eons by chance magma flows and frozen in the iron of an adamant dialectic.

He had begun to view without blinders the century's increasing witness to the experiment's dark side, to the no longer repressible facts of the tried and failed utopia. Wherever socialism was installed, there were barbed-wire camps, where "re-education of the exploiting classes" was but one of a hundred horrific euphemisms for the extermination of people — without distinction. The evidence of the vast Soviet and Asian archipelagos of human destruction was no longer dismissable as the aberrant tyranny of a single leader, the residuum of atavistic national habits that would themselves be gradually eliminated, for the gulags multiplied themselves wherever the experiment spread.

Were these terrible impulses that accompanied the century's revolutions not instead built-in — the unsuspected end-station of the materialist train? A growing dread had settled upon Degler in the turning world. A great blood dream hung over his sleep of an immense curtain suspended in dark folds upon the horizon of a vast plain. Over the plain, the masses of man were advancing, holding aloft icons on which one saw intelligent bearded faces with glittering eyes. But in the eyes of the men and women moving on the plain, there was a terrible fear. The people knew they were not marching to the light.

II

On the other side of the continent, Mavis Dawn took a break from posing in the new striped body-stocking to ponder the other side of her life: the Movement, the Change — the Revolution, actually.

Just now, that meant "No to Nukes!"

It was gaining ground. Was it ever! Just when all seemed darkest, when a self-appointed "truth squad" of nuke scientists reminiscent of the worst of the Fifties, had organized to follow along behind her own announced tour of the cities to speak out against the power plant nukes.

She had had to cancel the whole thing. The scientists held, she realized, the technical cards.

How could a generalist, or anyone of compassion, succeed against the deadly priests of science, boring their methodical way through the biosphere... Hey! That was great! Boring their way through the biosphere intent on its rape and pollution.

But then came "Meltdown Island!"

It was the predicted Big Nuke. Mavis recalled the excitement, the moment of personal reaffirmation, as the nation paused to watch the drama unfold — not, actually, from the nuke site, where it was all sort of hidden, but rather as shown, and shown with impact, from the anchor desks.

The nuke scientists and the Government had tried to play it down, but they didn't succeed.

No, here was the nuclear time bomb that almost went off. It didn't really matter that it was a human error, not a design error, or that it was contained, no deaths, no injuries, only frightened people. That didn't matter, because now they were saying, she had told the rallies: Hey! Wait a minute! What are you trying to do to us and our children and humanity — all for your obscene profits!

Then . . . History'd come through again — *antithesis* — bringing us ever closer to Change, though she hadn't seen that at the time. The Government, paranoid in its nightmare that "the Russians are coming," had started up a war fever, unleashed all the nation's darker passions, the McCarthy-like hysteria, the trillion dollar buildup of nukes, alarming the socialist peoples just as they were getting on their feet economically. The Government had stopped all that with its cowboy macho, forcing the brave eastern nation to respond in kind.

Mavis pondered Communism, actually the real victor over the Nazis in World War II while the United States was mostly in the Pacific fighting off just another Capitalist power. Also, the Nazis were the product of Late Capitalism. She had that from Dustin Rhett, the new president of Acting Persons Concerned. Dustin had an M.A. in poly sci from U.S.C.

Mavis truly enjoyed deep thought, and surrendered herself to it now. How tragic that the past Russian leader had so added to the problem! Was he a sick man? Privately, Mavis was ambivalent about Stalin. The "Gulag Archipelago" might have existed, but it was exaggerated. *She* would provide no grist to the mill of fascist capitalist reaction, wherever it reared its ugly head, such as wrapped in the Red White and Blue.

Hey! better get the kinks out of *that* sentence, Mavis thought, as she returned to the set and lay down on her side, raising one beautiful leg up to thirty degrees. She saw that the cameraman got an eyeful. So would the camera.

She was working on a second edition of her book, "Mavis Dawn's Fitness Primer." Just as she perceived in the world of conservative dark forces an indivisibility of evil, so she saw an interconnection of all things progressive. These included, among other things, economic justice, social equality, good nutrition and a fit body.

The Primer recorded her odyssey out of the early, sexploitative films — when the industry's moguls had manipulated her — into the achievement of social and physical awareness. It then went on to several pages showing Mavis and other beautiful women stretched out in tights, illustrating fitness. Finally, the Primer turned to an economic-social-political-fitness agenda for society.

The reason for the second edition was that she had, of all things, overlooked nukes in the first — and just when nuclear disarmament was beginning to come on! How could she have been so stupid! A second reason was: she wanted better resolution in some of the poses.

Between takes, Mavis worked out further her ideas for the Statement she intended to make at the fundraiser.

She was at her best in the "discovery" pose, her favorite self image. This pose had been captured best at the dramatic meeting with Nikki Boulanger that had set her future course. Nikki Boulanger was the young Black Communist professor whom the California Regents could not legally hinder from teaching political science to their children through a Leninist strainer.

Just right, the camera had caught Mavis' classic pout and starstruck expression. Something magical and profound had passed from the pretty Black professor to the beautiful actress: a discovery — of social sisterhood. "Discovery" hung prominently in all Mavis' residences, an earnest of her link to the revolutionary pantheon and History's heroic high circle.

She pondered the image you always saw of Lenin, the white and shining demigod, the features heroic and fine, charismatic, eternal. It had given to her the Statement's idea — a white and shining "goddess" — the face admired the world over by the spread of her films. A white statue, naked, its beauty explicit in all detail, to make every man desire, every woman envy. It would be . . . disinhibiting, revolutionary!

Once she had seen a very realistic, life-size statue of a woman she knew, the wife of one of those wealthy, guilt-ridden grocery chain magnates who hedged their bets by contributing to progressive causes. The wife had modelled for the statue, which stood in naked beauty true to every hue and cleavage in the middle of a grand boudoir. It was the first thing you saw when you stepped out of the house elevator into their bedroom. They'd take you up there without any warning, just to watch your reaction. Now I know what you *really* are like, the men smiled. You are *very* beautiful, said their girlfriends and wives.

III

Millikin was the youngest bishop in the country and the most dramatically photogenic without rival. While still a young priest, he had for a period worn fire-engine-red robes and stood out in the aisle, "in the round" as best one could in the traditional naves that pointed to the otherworldly, and he had spoken with fervor of peace, social justice, and economic equality. The anachronistic stained glass, he had hung over with banners proclaiming these same slogans, and in his improvised "round" he played a guitar, while a pretty girl sang "The Universal Soldier," or "Where Have All the Flowers Gone?" He had learned to speak quietly, with force and intensity, of man's social responsibility and of the sacredness of a rice bowl, a machete, and yes, a Kalashnikov.

One burning vision had come to consume him in the Protest Years. He called his vision "the intensest of light, hottest of fires."

By this, he meant nuclear weaponry, the crime against all history.

It began for him with the individual terrifying things. Napalm and burning villages, blackened hospital ruins, the sacrificial human torches. As the decade of protest accelerated, he had, one summer, bought Sterno cans and sat the parish youth at the doors with placards, behind the burning jelly, staring over the blue and yellow flames into the distraught faces of the arriving parishoners.

The fires of hell, for Millikin, were earthly fires and heaven's joys the earthly task. God was the Supreme Idea, man's ultimate possibility. The Church had funded these distillations of his doctoral study and their fermentation in Millikin's conviction that, ahead and no longer distant in time lay the epochal synthesis of the social and spiritual. History trended towards that great convergence, for whose completion the Church had much to ready — through dialogue, social action, and where necessary, revolution.

He dreamed a frequent dream. There was somewhere growing up, perhaps in America, a young boy or girl who would realize the convergence, would be the Church's greatest figure since Aquinas, perhaps since the man Jesus, who would build cathedrals not to God and the next life, but structures to terrestial man, wall-less, windowless cathedrals in the round, communitarian, encompassing,

multiple in truth, unhierarchical, not burdened by insti-
tutional wealth, egalitarian—a church not of God, but of
Man.

There would be no division in the Church in the round
as each looked upon each and not upon a dead symbology
of glass and stone. The nostalgic, the stubborn, the spiri-
tually infant—these would receive comfort and guidance
in places where such services could be efficiently concen-
trated.

In the new church, man would mature to his destiny
and would end his dream-myth of a savior, a forgiving father, a transcendent spirit. He would know a new nature.
This church would yield social man.

Out of his desk, the Bishop drew the magazine he had
bought that morning at the usual price of a smirk from
the newstand operator. Leaving the centerfold for a later
glance, he turned to the article illustrated by fiery mushroom clouds.

The clouds resulted, he summarized it for memory,
from certain things his own government did from time to
time. In fact, the Government had so many nuclear warheads that the new cloud type posed the threat of sup-
planting the earth's natural cloud cover at the push of a
button. The reasons for this insanity, though complex, had
mostly to do, the article said, with a Wisconsin senator
of many years ago, with a persistent nationalistic paranoia, and with a certain five-sided office building. Bishop
Millikin inferred that the mushrooms were a peculiarly
American problem.

True, the other side had warheads and could produce similar cosmic catastrophe. But it had been driven to this desperate state and to ever higher arms levels out of fear of the Bishop's government. Accompanying the article was an interview with the director of the American Institute of that country. Orlov was a fat, relaxed fellow who looked like a tired, good-natured Ohio politician. The major problem inserting itself between our two great peoples, the Ohio politician said, was the United States' unpredictability.

Millikin nodded assent and, maintaining firm discipline, flipped the pages undiverted to the book reviews. Here were two relevant pieces on the nation's arms build-up. One made the case for a bloodlessly efficient military out of control, the other for a grossly inefficient military out of control. Millikin agreed with both. Then, having read the magazine for the reasons purchased, he opened it to the middle and spread out the centerfold.

Millikin had never satisfactorily resolved the question: should a priest read The Magazine? He meditated on the case of the Episcopalian churchman in California, who not only proclaimed that he read it, but had published an article in it on the Church and Open Marriage.

The Magazine certainly had seen an evolution since its defensive early mission work in behalf of the sexual revolution. The constrained risque had graduated inexorably and inch by fleshly inch over the years from pert and pretty rumps, to full frontal, to parted thighs— the Bishop swallowed— to masturbatory suggestion.

Certainly The Magazine's "philosophy" had self-realized itself, too. Now, one could read without hang-up of animal sex, and sex "face to fork" — this position was said to be "experience at its most direct and pure."

But one read The Magazine for its cultural daring, not as a register of the general advance of pornography — to use that dated moralism. As a matter of fact, Millikin recalled, it was in these pages that he had read of Shannon, the novelist of demon possession, now richer than a king and patron of Change. Sitting atop his pile, Shannon had written of the fictional uses of irony. Perhaps "Demons" had brought us all to realize the darkness of the depths of unquestioned religious faith. "Demons" had brought us face to fork with the consequences of adherence to moral absolutes.

Shannon's was a heartening example of the Church's emboldened self-critique — lay and clergy. Millikin was also well aware of the increasing literature by and about what used to be called, and he winced, "the Religious." Everywhere you looked, renounced Fathers and liberated nuns were declaring independence, marrying each other, writing bold revelations for the literary magazines. It had become almost a cliche: "Jacqueline Jacqueline, who has taught American literature in high schools in New England, is a former Sister of Mercy."

And they all went at the Church with a vengeance. Why? Did the Church fail them? Or had it, perhaps, failed to convince them — of its own relevance to the world of Change? Wasn't the social sector the supreme relevance today? The Church richly deserved the radical critique it was getting — Millikin believed that firmly. One had to consider its complicity, in every era down to the present, in sheer, raw, human exploitation. Millikin's advanced degree was in sociology, the discipline that he regarded as a lens of light, the correcting mirror to history's deep and vast deceptions.

IV

There had not been time for a sculpture, but the molding process, which she had suffered through, naked, and uneasily — all she could think of was death masks — had produced near perfection. Mavis threw the canvas off the statue.

She was beautiful as a goddess is beautiful at the instant of creation, standing white on the pedestal, hipshod, arms hanging palms out, the face lovely, its expression expectant: "discovery." Eve in joy of Adam, Degler thought. "Wow!" he said. Mavis smiled. Shannon frowned. "Will you pick up the color?" he asked.

Mavis signalled to the technicians, and they darkened the mirrored room. Out of the blackness, in the twinkling of an eye, Mavis appeared in perfect natural skin tints and hair color. The film imagers were precise to the line, the color exact — the fine dark blonde hair, the eyes bright blue, the skin rosy through a light tan, the peach-pink of the lips and . . . In the darkness, Degler gasped. Next to him, Mavis laughed merrily.

The goddess began to speak about the body, the people, peace, and the planet. "That's good," Shannon said. "Moving." Degler did not hear what the goddess was saying. What he was seeing seemed to him more beautiful than all life, beauty in its purest image. He watched, un-distracted by the message from the moving lips, lost in the animation of the classic features, staring unselfconsciously at the beautiful body that seemed to him beauty's own revelation.

"Now, brace yourself," said the other Mavis.

A pale yellow light began gradually to bathe the form now fallen silent. Mavis' features had assumed a sugges-tion of concern, the faintest hint of fear. The light intensi-fied. In a few moments, it became quite harsh. Emotion began to animate the face as the light brightened. The fear that rose in Mavis' eyes passed by stages into a gather-ing terror. The light reddened, grew brilliant, brightened to intensest white. In the mushroom of blinding light, the features of the statue were no longer distinguishable.

Gradually the intense light lessened, darkening in waves that washed over the indistinct face and form. But a dark figure began now to emerge in detail, and its features were horrifying. The love-woman was a torn and charred burning skeleton. Blood surged from the sockets of what had been Mavis' eyes. Bone protruded through the black-ened flesh. Degler's hair stood on end. *Verwoeste . . . Verwo este Stad* , torso-torn Rotterdam burning in the death-rain.

"Great! Great!" Shannon cried. "My 'Demons' make-up guys are amazing! Prima! Mavis, you are a genius!"

"Hiroshima, mon Amour," Mavis said.

V

In the next days, Degler completed his calls. There was no

doubt that the fundraiser "statement" was stirring wide curiosity. "What will she do—deep knee bends?" somebody joked. It's about Give Peace a Chance, and it will be dramatic, he told them.

On the final weekend, "Throat" noted the upcoming occasion in the morning *Press*. "There may be a surprise guest at the royal gala at 'Hollywood East'," Throat hinted. "Not a king, but a bishop."

Millikin had accepted—joyfully, Degler thought. He'd spoken with him personally after talking to the Bishop's secretary, a priest who, Degler decided, could make it in the political world any day. The Bishop could, too, for that matter.

It was easy also to engage Orlov. The Russian accepted even before asking the date. He'd perhaps better not contribute the "door fee," Orlov suggested—"to avoid somebody's paranoia." No, of course not, Degler said.

The others were more difficult. Organizers only rarely reached important people directly. You had to approach through layers—assistants, law partners, friends, activist grandmothers. Degler made the political contacts, but in the end it was Mavis, operating out of Shannon's place, who reached most of the celebrities. Degler wished he owned the priceless numbers list. Hardest of all to reach were the environmentalists, some of them days away by backpack.

The focus, of course, was on those empowered to vote on resolutions and budgets, most of these being in the party for which Degler worked. For the ones who found attendance steep, he arranged funding through the National Committee, which said unquestionably yes.

The Committee was more concerned about other problems at the moment. It was, in fact, plainly worried about the mounting depredations of the so-called "high-tech conservatives." This improbable term described a cell of madcap young Silicon Valley engineers, some of the new yuppie millionaires evidently, who were keeping Security and Communications paranoid. There were now clear indications, for example, that these twisted techies had video-compromised the Committee's whole strategy to lock up the Black vote. The cynical tapes had been received by Black leaders in several cities, with as yet unknown consequences for the congressional elections.

You had to expect anything. There was technology today that made the Watergate capers look like Indian smoke signals. Tiny scan cameras, sensors, image relayers, fibre optics transmission, and remoted image broadcast of a resolution so fine that Degler had only to recall Mavis' production to visualize the stunning realism.

Not that there were any flies on the Committee in this department. Degler recalled the paralyzing "tricks" he had himself helped organize. These were voice-over re-tapes on which opposition Senators enunciated various idiocies and racial slurs. They had had the tapes circulated out of the universities — the apparent products of ingenious student hi-jinks. Democracy!

VI

By the end of the final week, nearly everything was in place. Degler called up his sister, who taught Middle Ages and Reformation at the university. Ann was glad to see him, cheerful even though the children had left to spend the holidays with their father.

Ann did not take seriously his atheism or his two and a half cheers for socialism. You are too intelligent to be an Illedge, she said. Degler had in fact known few atheists of the professing sort who did not remind him of the nasty little crank in *Point Counterpoint*. Ann laughed without mocking him at "the most dismal face of the physiognomy of angst."

"That just isn't your face," she said.

Degler recalled for her the *heroic* moderns — Trotsky, Rosa Luxemburg, Sartre — all good names, Stalin's brutalities having made the Prophet Unarmed an enduring socialist saint. But I'll make them keep Aquinas for you, he told her. You couldn't live without your precarious "cathedral of intellect." No, you'll keep Loyola, she'd said. Loyola is the model for your century's totalist saints.

She insisted, and he gave in, and they went to a "Messiah sing-along" in the cathedral. He hoped no one would see him, notwithstanding the deafening clatter that had been set off by the epidemic fall of ironic smiles in the remarkable quadrennium not far back, titularly led by a devout believer. It had become in bad taste to snicker about religion, and around the city one witnessed unlikely displays of public reverence. Prominent figures, not before faith-professing, bowed their heads, even squinted shut their eyes, lipping whispered amens.

There was even some suggestion that the phenomenon, whatever its origins, was not just a passing one. Degler had a wary sense of a creeping back of the metaphysical. Nor was it limited to the choreographed grotesqueries of the electronic church pitchmen. There was, for example, in fiction today the suggestion of a new tendency — to counterpoise "values," old against new, and to resurrect moral categories, and even to question the very idea of relativism — the orbit of the whole wobbly century. It was said now that the Samoan girls had been pulling Margaret Mead's leg, and she never knew it. In short stories, one encountered, if ever so occasionally, an unapologetic religosity. But beyond all comprehension for Degler was the sounding claim of the Soviet dissidents that the authorities in Russia could not stop the resurgent interest in religion.

Solzhenitsyn: the dangerous exaggerations of the overwrought and antimodernist zealot whom Degler had never read. Yet the Gulag's most famous inmate had, he knew, touched a nerve in the modern psyche, East and West. And this despite the reviews that had so deftly separated the artist from the would-be prophet, the sufferer from the flawed system, the still-true socialist ideal from "Stalinism." Solzhenitsyn and the other throwbacks to pre-1917 had had the temerity found only in reactionaries to state a *moral* position "from under the rubble."

Here was the most stupendous irony — the revival of belief in the oldest core of the materialist heartland. And

Degler stood again baffled before the dialectic's lurch, vast beyond all grasp.

He was approaching the cathedral, and his eye was taken as always by the scale and majestic line of its great white presence.

This inapt word he had long since stopped avoiding, because if he had stopped using it, he would have had instead to employ some metaphor incompatible with his view of all the earth as material only.

In "presence," he recognized the distinction he drew between the cathedral and every other sheltering structure. The cathedral was a last symbol, displaced in time, of the Age of Faith, when on uncounted sites throughout Christendom the community united in an enterprise that transcended generations and whose great architects were anonymous, to build heavenward — enclosing vaster interior space than man ever had before, discovering new structural principles, new uses and textures of light, new heights of faith. And each of the great Gothic churches — Chartres, Rheims, Ulm, Prague — was unique in the line and form of schiff, buttress, and spire. Each had, like no other, a particularity of nave and transept, clerestory and choir, of stained glass and statuary, the detail everywhere, even in the great heights where only God's eye, or Quasimodo's, could see it, until the Baedekers and binoculars of the nineteenth century rediscovered the majesty and order of the High Medieval.

She surprised him standing like a pilgrim before the unfinished towers, and she laughed as she took his arm and pulled him into the converging crowds. They passed through the high doors like small children and through the fore chambers into the deep nave, its great space a softness of light richly textured by the sun through the brilliant glass.

It seemed that it took only moments to fill, and at once the grand oratorio began, encompassing and embracing every material body, living and stone without distinction. They rose with their librettos to the ascending chorales, Ann singing, as he watched her happily, with an unselfconscious joy. But Degler was singing, too—and he could not sing—singing mightily and with all his heart. He could not separate himself from the surging music that rose about him into the heights of the nave.

He was singing in a sea of light, a suffusing light surging with the music, light pure, whole, expanding. He felt a pouring of light around him without dimension. The universe was light in an infinite diversity of mood and texture, crystal light so pure that he wanted to cry with joy above the crescendo, light diffused yet heavy on the deep world, illuminating the life that was everywhere. The light was living, creating all that he could see and the infinitude that he did not see and that was flowing by him, not to return, each image infinite in depth and complexity, unique in place and time, an emanation of the coursing change half-seen.

Degler saw that the streaming beauty he perceived, accidental in its passing, yet flowing uniquely for him like no stream of light beheld by any other of the thousand millions of men and women in that instant of time, that this incomprehensible flow of being consisted of glimmers

only, and that he was beholding but a pinpoint of the infinite beauty of the light. And he began to realize that he
had come face on to the fact of the utter fullness of the light
and that it existed in unfathomed dimension. The world's
deep reached beyond all bound, and the unbounded light
was God.

They went afterwards to dinner at a place overlooking
the river, descending gradually from the majestic Handel
chorales. "Magical," Degler said to Ann. "Mystical," she
corrected him.

She had to leave then for a seminar. I can find my way
out, she told him, so he stayed awhile watching the pattern of the night in the moving lights beyond the river.

He could not keep from his mind the vision of unbounded light. Within it, the dread fireball, inspiration to
the gathering force of Mavis' grand cause, was the tini-
est pinpoint of the power of one small sun in the limitless
reaches of the light. In no way was it a "totality" blanketing
every human concern, as he had heard the Bishop declare
with intensity to the obsequious, blinking hosts of the talk
shows. Nor did the fireball "submerge concepts that we no
longer quite look upon as absolutes." Could Hiroshima,
any more than any event in history render meaningless
that which showed itself in the pouring of the light upon
the squinted vision of the world? Had modern memory
indeed been stamped unalterably by the hellish violence
of the Great War, so that all beauty's imagery had become
tainted, tinted indelibly in some sepia hue that colored
over the world's browning, whimpering end?

No, the light that animated the universe was the

abounding reality beyond the accumulating horrors of
his century: the worldwide span of war, the extermination centers introducing the industrialization of killing,
the encompassing lethality of the Gulag, the socialist leaps
forward over mountains of corpses, the studied and sys-
tematic destruction of culture and memory in holocausts
encompassing whole peoples, the slaughter of the never-
born in the antiseptic clinics of nations that once had held
that life sacred.

All these stupendous enormities that were smothering
the darkening century, all were more dreadful than was
the threat of nuclear battle, and they, unlike it, were on the
terrible record of the twentieth century. Where were the
signs that they were abating? That metaphor of Millikin's,
the "intensest of light, hottest of fires," the nuclear metaphor for rational civilization's ineluctable self-destruction,
was itself no more than the latest exercise in the politics of
fear. No, the world was not being destroyed by fire or per-
il of fire. It was rotting of itself, for in the very heart of the
great civilization that had held it together, it was losing,
with accumulating rapidity, its sense of the sacred. In the
now profoundly materialist West, the formula for progress was an unquestioned and unbounded egalitarianism.
But this formula, in the uninterrupted journey to its logical
end, was breaking down the very values of hierarchy, family, and individuality that sustained the institutions standing against the great winds of power. The socialist lands
were a foretaste of that rampaging power that moved like
a giant earth-scraping machine over the old and tended
landscape, blading the masses of humanity into an equal-

ity as uniform as the "Asiatic social formation" that Marx had recognized in the ancient worker-states, but had taken pains to exclude from his dialectic of human history. Out of the mirror of the ages flashed a hideous reflection to engage the all-questioning mind of modernity.

Beyond all the winds of power — those of the materialist century's typhonic egoism, and those swirling chiliastic dreams through time of the earth's utopia — beyond these existed the transcending and limitless choirs of light beyond measure.

VII

They were beginning to arrive, and Millikin stood in a vestibule looking down with whetted appetite at the alighting celebrities. Like sleek salmon, they were ascending Shannon's cascades to the nets of the fishers of men within.

Degler arrived just behind a sparkling run of Hollywood folk, whose capped teeth smiles fairly lit up the way to the Oscar at the door. Stationed at his Versailles portals, Shannon greeted them all in a stagy style that revealed the swift passage from writer's muse to show biz to be complete.

Degler was astonished at the diverse parade of self-conscious class he witnessed in the next hour: a former United States Senator with a household name — Seventies victim of the vox populi, a once Secretary of State who held his head like DeGaulle, a Black poetess of rage, a blonde anchorwoman with challenging eyes. There was a managing editor of a newspaper with national pretensions, a Southern novelist who couldn't go home again, and a *New Yorker* storywriter "atune as no one else to social disjunctions and the discontinuity of relationships." Orlov was ubiquitous through the house, courting the junior congressmen for whom Degler had been paid to flood Mavis' political occasion.

Looking around, Degler thought he recognized, gold cross on hairy chest, the director of the pathbreaking film about the chainsaw swamp murders. Staging a grand entrance, turning every head, was Dustin Rhett, who had flown in directly from the Big Sky Country piloting his own jet. Rhett lived and wrote on a secluded ranch with spectacular views of the roof of the continent and reachable only by horse or helicopter, from which vantage he pled for the restricted use of the Western wilderness before man destroyed it.

"Any serious Christian must be a socialist," Millikin heard himself say, repeating the aphorism of a postwar theologian—not of the Church, actually, but one of "theirs."

"Super!" Mavis exclaimed. Millikin saw that his shining-eyed hostess took "Christian socialist" for a Millikin original, and, possibly, a new Church position.

"Oh, I am *into* the worker-priests!" said Mavis. "And the murdered nuns." With professional polish, she transformed her unbounded admiration into an air of tragic concern for the summary symbol of all the repressive free-market regimes of Latin America.

Degler stood with the knot of people that had gathered

around Mavis and the Bishop. Were the missionary organizers people of Christ, or of a prophet more modern? Or,
of both? Degler had visited a New England monastery of
the Order, gauging Church sentiment early during the last
campaign. They'd invited him to the midday meal. They
all ate in silence, The Rule, while a Brother read. The reading was not from Saint Francis or Augustine, however, but
from a historical classic, the reader said, about ten days in
1917 that shook the world.

"Nukes," Mavis was saying. "The nukes are the preem-
inent moral issue today. Don't we agree, Bishop Millikin?"
Then she placed her hand on the Bishop's and struck the
pose that Degler recognized as the Nikki Boulanger special. "And may I call you Jim?"

"Yes, we agree . . . and, of course!" Millikin said, en-
chanted and excited. What a woman! He kept smiling.

Mavis now grasped and squeezed both the Bishop's
hands. Inclining her head to one side, she beheld him
through a new expression meant to convey, Degler was
sure, the adoration of the innocent.

Millikin's exclamation came from the soul. At that moment, he did not know whether, in the next instant, he
would not go dancing hand-in-hand through the room
with Mavis Dawn. But he regained composure almost
at once and began then to talk fervently to his new and
beautiful protege. How quick her responses, how bright,
informed!

The light from the mirrors magnified the electric evening that coursed about the mystery statue standing mid-
way along one wall, its tightly secured canvas defeating

all attempted sneak previews. Degler moved away from the Church Temporal toward a group gathered around a man who was talking like a woman. Have we here, Degler wondered, the stuff of the social novel of our time? "Robin Bite, who cross-dresses brilliantly, sends us the freshest bulletin from the front: what is happening out there on the androgynous edge, all of us eager to snatch it up."

Teddy Tedesco, Mavis' rival on the morning exercise circuit, held court wide-eyed and all little boy from an elegant couch, leg tucked up under. The rhythm of his speech and gesture was consciously feminine. About him stood a fragmentary semicircle listening to the patter with steady goodwill. Degler caught the flicker of annoyance in Mavis' glance across the room.

Looking back at Tedesco, Degler thought of his nephews, now on their holiday trip to California to see Daddy, an affluent gynecologist in Marin. For the Doctor, Ann's second pregnancy—precarious and requiring "self-denial"— had signalled the "today" of—Today is the First Day of the Rest of Your Life. The rest of the Doctor's life was proceeding with a second wife, a former stewardess, the first wife having been "outgrown." Daddy let them watch the "naughty channel," the boys told Degler, and the gay couple next door— "really crazy guys"—came by to watch, too.

"We have our hawks, you have your hawks," the anchorwoman was saying to the Russian. Orlov's face was a complex of happy creases. Orlov understood the Americans. He smiled all the time.

"The Russians are coming, the Russians are here," said

Mavis, joining them. "When *are* you coming to 'get' us, Sergei?"

"Oh, choost any time now," the Russian said.

In the anchorwoman's mind, Mavis' witticism stirred a related thought. It was the pithy aphorism of a lovable little comic-strip animal, cited often during Vietnam. "Yes, 'we have met the enemy'," she said, smiling at Mavis. " 'And . . . he is *us!* " Orlov smiled with new creases. A favorite joke of the Americans.

Close by, the Black poetess was loosing her rage with relish on the suffering flesh of the Southern novelist. The novelist's greatest work, a cry of antebellum guilt seen through updated eyes and a Manhattan perspective, had nonetheless demeaned, in its stereotyping, all Black women, the poetess said. "I spilled my Southern guts for Blacks!" the novelist cried in agony. "No, m— —-f— —-," she said, "you humanized crackerland and your proto-fascist forebears."

Degler moved on and out of earshot of the Southern seminar. A last group filtered in, completing his mental list and fulfilling the fundraiser's heavy take. Should he stay to see the "statement" again? He decided that there had to be some kind of historian, even a lapsed one, on hand to witness what surely would go down as a milestone in the annals of Hollywood self-display.

People were ascending and descending Shannon's grand circular stair in a steady flow. Degler observed that the women invariably came down the vertical stage more slowly. As he watched, Mavis, descending, turned into view, lingering a moment above the room soon to be treated to her best-guarded secret. Nude descending — he couldn't help it. But Mavis had not paused to invite attention, she was looking for someone. Degler followed her eye to the striking figure of the Bishop.

Now he joined again the circle that had attended Millikin through most of the evening. The Bishop was clearly the evening's star, speaking quietly, with eloquence, to the concerned intelligent faces that turned constantly towards his own. He returned to each this adulation — it was his gift, and his fine warm smile, accenting each idea with compassion, opened every yielding mind.

For Degler, as he stood listening to Millikin, the charisma overspanned an intellectual chaos. Here, in the social-priest, was that mindset — contemptuous of history — that was oblivious even of its own origins. Millikin had not one farthing's grasp of economics. The Bishop gazed upon the running sores of human cultures millennia-old and diagnosed the bacillus as capitalism, the malady, American.

In the bizarre and kaleidoscopic evening, so dominated by an unalleviated cycnicism, Degler was struck by the fragmented character of contemporary society. That steady shattering of objective value that one encountered in the salons of the age seemed to him to be the main current of modern life. But he was shaken — and how did this happen to one who had renounced faith — by the falling of the mortar from the oldest grand edifice of that society, the basis of all tradition, the spiritual and psychological foundation now trembling on the bedrock of the world. The Church, as it had so often in its long centuries and always to its sustaining harm, had again entered the political realm, had descended from the transcendent high truths sensed by every generation to the mocking salons of power to prove itself by the values of others, no longer confident in its own.

The Bishop was a recurring archetype, the political priest, a commonplace in history, assured as each of his sort that he was leading the Church to its rational terrestial completion. And so he had altogether lost a sense of what the Church had believed was the original completion, the central event in time that Pasternak had called the only true revolution in human history — the revelation to each individual soul that compelled every man and woman to confront in unshadowed light their nature, their helplessness, and their dependence on the light that comprehended the darkness of their being.

Wasn't it this very relationship that defined every individual, each unique in his time and in all historical time? And that uniqueness was the most profound fact of existence. In the collective trend of modern life, the individual had no definition. Just read the Marxist historians, Degler thought. All the tenets of the twentieth century were keyed to the material ground of personality, to the submergence of the individual in a thickening social porridge in which the age sought to read the meaning and end of history. And in the material vision, there were no universal ideas transcending time, true for every man and woman, when each idea, relative in history, had its season, only to give way before the inexorable dialectic.

Yet some principles within the scheme of Millikin's vision were absolute. "The People," Degler heard the Bishop enjoin his enthralled circle, "the People, not you, not I, will write the future. The 'individual,' defined by 'liberty', is nothing other than a bourgeois bubble in time. Equality — across all human boundaries — and those boundaries will be erased — equality, radical and true, is the defining and absolute force that is going to save this planet from the intensest of light, hottest of fires."

VIII

The gala was gradually drawing to its focus. From throughout the glass palace and up out of the wine cellars the prime hybrid of both coasts was converging on the Versailles room. The last roamers descended from the upper floors and joined the widening semicircle around the draped figure.

The chatter died down as Mavis emerged in front of the statue.

"We came here tonight," she announced. "For a purpose. You have been generous for peace, and you are beautiful!" Degler tugged at his earlobe involuntarily.

"We desire passionately the end of the nuclear nightmare," Mavis continued. "The end of the balance of terror. We want an absolute freeze on nukes by the Government, the government that first in all the world threatens peace by its arrogance of power — the American Government."

Degler thought it was remarkable that the smiling man standing next to him was the distinguished former Senator — now a wealthy Washington lawyer — who had sloganized "arrogance of power" only a few years ago.

Back then, Mavis' budding ambitions had run to the excitement of man sexually rather than politically, Degler considered. She would certainly double the action tonight.

" . . . a *Statement ,*" Mavis was saying. "That I wanted personally to make, a statement that transcends me, my body, my feelings."

"*It ,*" she said. "*It* will be our destiny, *if peace fails .*"

"We *must ,*" Mavis said fervently, "*surrender to peace*"!

The crowd went into an expectant buzz as Mavis left the room. Shannon, moving efficiently, prevented several of his guests from descending again to the bars. From his post in the rear, Degler looked around the semicircle. Where was Millikin?

The effect upon him of this *woman* was a thing that Millikin had never before experienced, and the excitement he felt on their meeting, she had whetted to unfamiliar keenness through the evening. He found that she watched him constantly, smiling over someone's shoulder, or from the mirrors, and occasionally as he met her eyes, his quiet earnest sermons faltered. He found himself now and again searching her out in the multiple panorama of the mirrored room.

Millikin had been conscious of his effect on girls and women since first chased down for kisses after baseball games, and he had not easily overcome The Problem in his novice years. But now the Bishop was feeling the fire of "the sexual dimension" that he had all his adult life kept in the abstract. There was no mistaking Mavis' overtures, and when in the middle of the evening she had endeavored to spirit him away from his admirers to show him Shannon's upper rooms—the stereo studio and tiny theater, the palatial sunken baths and jacuzzi deck, Shannon's secluded study with sliding panels, the ladder-like eighteenth-century stairs to an isolated high sleeping loft—she had told him that she wanted him, and he was unsurprised.

He waited for her at the Statement's given hour. You and I will make our *personal* statement, she'd said. And now she appeared and guided him to the highest and deepest place in the house.

Three stories below, Shannon looked about, puzzled, then at his watch, and, after some hesitation, signalled the technicians. The light in the Versailles room dimmed, and a hush fell again over the crowd. It became finally quite dark. The canvas rustled. The pedestaled goddess appeared in brilliant white light. In a few moments, just as suddenly, Mavis assumed color and life, naked and beautiful in sensuous detail.

She spoke of giving peace a chance, of making love not war, of giving a war and no one coming, of flowers not bombs, of nukes and profits, of a nation no longer corrupted by the religion of growth and greed. She spoke of the autonomy of a woman's body, about life and how it all came together in your body, my body. "I am life," she said, Mavis, the lips parting, the starstruck eyes, the crescendo of feeling spreading suffusing warmth through the beautiful body. "Life!" she cried.

High in the wall behind him, Degler heard very faintly a brief series of clicks. Abruptly, the room went dark. But the imagers seemed to recover almost instantly. Light again bathed the naked form of Mavis. Hiroshima time, Degler murmured.

But Mavis was not "yellowing." Nor were her features conveying subtle transitions. Her face was undergoing rapidly a horrible transformation. It was darkening, contorting, distending into ugly bulging flesh. The lips grew very thick, twisting over feral teeth. From the black eye sockets, slitted pupils shifted rapidly over the frozen audience. From the monstrous head came a deep guttural stream of obscenities. Standing in the first circle of the horrified watchers, Shannon began to scream.

Abruptly, the fiend-head jerked sideways, began slowly to turn, turned in the socket of Mavis' shoulders completely backwards. At that moment, a violent scream sounded from high in the house, and a shattering *crack* went through the Versailles room from end to end.

Recoiling from the writhing figure on the bed, Millikin screamed from the pain of a searing fire over the whole front of his body. As he staggered backwards, the figure leaped upon him, and they fell headlong together down the steep ladder stair.

The party broke up in a frantic confusion. Women shouted hysterically, men screamed. Shannon lay unrevived at the foot of the white statue, its head smashed in pieces beside him. Every mirror in the room lay in shards on the floor. What in the hell was this, Dustin Rhett shouted—a prank of Shannon's to promote another run on his awful book? "Crass!" the storywriter shouted with care, "the most vicious kind of right-wing joke genre." Cut slightly on the face by the glass, the Secretary of State left, dabbing his wound above the confusion. The Senator and the panicked congressmen jostled their way through the frantic crowd erupting onto the street.

The arriving police drove everybody out of the house, grabbing witnesses from among the rapidly decamping guests. "No, nobody's going back in there tonight," the cop told Degler over his protests. "Not until we find out just what in holy hell happened in that place."

The story did not appear in the morning's *Press*. The managing editor declined to find newsworthy the details of a story either so idiotic in outcome or else of the genre of the mass hysterical. Nor did the anchors, the following evening, find any news value in the embarassing social affair. But the tabloids published eyewitness accounts that went throughout the country, and by the end of the week, supermarket sackstuffers carried the lurid event, with artists' renderings, to the last illiterate.

The facts that came to light the next morning — confirmed by police inspection, and Degler's — were these: Mavis Dawn lay with broken neck at the foot of a steep stair on the fourth floor of Shannon's house. In repose, she was not beautiful. Her head had been wrenched almost completely around by the violence of the fall, and her swollen, discolored features were hardly recognizable. Next to her nude body, and also nude, lay the unconscious form of James X. Millikin, bishop of the see of a Southern city and a well known peace activist. Every mirror in the fundraiser room lay in splinters and shards on the floor. Shannon, violent and incoherent, had had to be straight-jacketed.

Degler left the house in the afternoon, as the police locked and posted Shannon's door. One of them duct-taped a police notice directly over the Academy Award. Degler's eye shifted to the door of the adjoining house. "Technical Creations" was gone!

There was no listed telephone, but a day later Degler located the agent who leased the house. "I don't know who they were," he told Degler. "They just wanted it for a month, and they paid me double what I said. It sure hasn't been easy renting this place after 'Demons'."

The Movement took pains to distance itself from the unfortunate affair. After some negotiation and through the offices of Dustin Rhett, Degler turned over the whole fund-raiser take to the League to Save the Western Timberwolf. Bishop Millikin retreated, following a long hospital stay, into the arms of the Church, into one of those cloistered havens in the California mountains, where the treatment is mainly medieval and where the roses are tended and the world may be wonderfully complete within the eye's range.

HOMO LIBERALIS

They forgot where they came from.
They lost sight of what brought them
along . . . . The mockers came.
And the deniers were heard.

— Carl Sandburg

I

It was a lovely Memorial Day morning, and Dr. Beers was speaking to the veterans and their ladies. Magnolias, columns, the terraced lawn to the tidal river—it was all there—and when they pledged allegiance in their fervent Southern English, Beers stood as he must with hand over heart but moved his lips not at all. Not when there was not justice for *all*. And they sang America. Then they sang Dixie. And Lamm Beers placed his finger to his nostril.

The prisoner of war speech was invariably a hit.

The war and beginnings, Normandy and the young lieutenant. The night patrol that had deployed too far, and dawn too soon in the maze of hedgerows. The machine guns, his dead sergeant. Capture. The profound psychological shock—"For you, the war is over," the German officer had said. Then his breakdown before the men—the first and last of his captivity. The train east.

One morning they were passing through Koblenz, and they went by an ancient church. Over the wall, he saw a priest going about his cloistered everyday in this war of wars, loyal to the society that was gassing the six million.

East across Germany to remote Posen, to *Offizier Lager* 5, the prisoner of war camp for American ground army officers.

The hard regimen of the *Oflag* — but the Red Cross parcels came. And they made each other little gifts — a muffler, or a few cigarettes. He was never beaten or mistreated. Then the war's last chapter and evacuation westward before the victorious Soviet armies, on foot in the winter of the North German Plain, and he lost his gloves. But there were barns to sleep in at night.

The last day of the war was anticlimactic. "Now you are free," the British officer said. Yet the gaining of freedom was more traumatic than its loss had been. For with freedom, he left behind the prison of the past and stepped forth from the pyre of history into "a world without illusions."

He declared that his captivity had formed his fundamental view of life. He had seen the Total War and the Holocaust, and God was silent.

But this last, he deleted for today's audience. To the patriotic group he did not say that the War had collapsed forever the edifice of the old, had reduced it to cinder in the firestorms and the death ovens of its lethal superstitions.

He said instead that to the newer world he had pledged a life of compassion.

Compassion, and peace, and equality, and the oneness of all men. For he had seen in those last weeks in the German forests the eternal vision — the Shining Titan, towering over the wrecked cathedrals. Man, eternal self-creator, measure of all things.

He finished speaking and lowered his head. But even now, the demons were dancing. How he abominated that world destroyed, the world in whose crimes his own victorious nation was so inextricably joined.

Yet, for his nation he had hope — in a progressive union that would bring to the planet its destiny of social justice and equality, that would turn his nation's power and great wealth to the final and historic liberation of all men from the ancient tyrannies.

Carried away by the intenseness of his story and its mystic flight, the veterans broke into applause that was sudden as a thunderclap. Row by row they stood to ovation. They knew the suffering and the enduring and honored the eloquent hope they heard. And Beers, chin on chest, let the applause wash over him and was happy to the severed edges of his mind where he had in those final weeks of war cut his soul clean.

His captivity was the Event of his life, and he shared it often and with joy. Heroes who return from war are silent. Lamm Beers was eloquent in a vicarious role.

II

FROM HIS BIG leather chair, Beers looked over his half-glasses out the embrasure to the moat of the fort's sea front. Aimed at the wide opening, his desk commanded the same flanking field of fire across the granite wall as had the guns of the National Period.

In fact, a six pounder had exploded on this very spot in 1845, killing its whole crew. Beers raised his eyes to their ten-thousandth search for iron reminders in the pitted vaults and arches of his casemate office. Finding none, he refocused on the rising tide of the moat as he turned his mind to the problem at hand.

The problem was that he had lost two valuable men at once to the blossoming of a distant place in the organization, and the system had taken seven months to produce replacements. By that time, he had been ready to hire anyone sight unseen who knew the language.

About Jean Damon, already on board, he had no doubts. Damon was a short, fat, brilliant French Army authority, a Fulbright Fellow just returned from a year at the Sorbonne. He was already going great guns on the early "evil-war" volume.

But about Cheyenne he was less confident. His second new man had called just that morning from a school in the Rockies to say, in flat Western accents, that he would report inside a month.

It was true that Cheyenne had published and came with good credentials. But a shudder passed through Beers as he pondered the egregious *cultural rape* implied in his new assistant's name. More than that—here in all probability was a flag-waving, eagle-shooting Wyoming reactionary.

Around the corner of the far bastion swam a mother coot with her little family. Though well back from the open embrasure doors, Beers, from long birdwatcher habit, froze in place, training his sharp far vision on the fledglings, just feathering out. They would be flying soon, but here they were safe, for the old coastal fortress and its beachlands were also a bird refuge. Beers, an environmentalist, had helped get it designated. On the glass door of the bookcase behind his desk was displayed a bumper sticker, which read:

Open Season: Hunt a Hunter

When the coots had paddled out of sight, Beers rose to take his daily tour through the catacombs of the Institute archives.

Spread through the casemates and alcoved bastions of the old double tiered fort were the manuscript collections, book holdings, and combat documents of the nation's military history from Jamestown through Vietnam and beyond. Violence: an American institution, Beers mused. As American as apple pie. The cliches did not bother him — they were so blatantly true!

Bespectacled archive denizens hurried past Beers on the endless errands of their coded trade. Young and old, they skittered through the vaults like hunted men. Hunted they were, Beers knew. Miss Washington, their boss, was always near.

Miss Washington was a glaring five-foot minority whose rapid footfalls and quick sharp shouts signalled nearly every day some discovery of male goldbricking or jittery error. This morning, she had already caught prey in the Inchon casemate, and Beers took quick evasive action, stepping neatly through the Korean arch into the Vietnam bastion.

His own initial collision with Miss Washington had

been painful in the acute. Every time he thought of it, he imagined his blood was congealing. In fact, Beers remained baffled and stricken by the Black archivist's response to what he had intended as an expression of sensitive solicitude. He'd wanted her to know about his own Black Friend, whom he entertained each year as a houseguest.

"*Black* friend?" Miss Washington's smile had dripped wickedness. "Why, I thought liberals were colorblind!" she'd said.

Miss Washington, who was unaccountably a Republican, had sealed this insolence by calling Beers' favorite Black leader, once a U.N. ambassador, a "Black racist." "He thinks he's an *African!*" she'd snorted.

Black or no Black, Miss Washington was a vicious little feist and unmitigated ingrate. Late in life, Lamm Beers concluded that, though he loved Blacks in the mass, he could hate an individual Black as intensely as he could any redneck.

The quick deployment out of the Inchon hotspot brought Beers into the cavernous chambers of All Evil. Looking around, he observed with no joy how the swollen holdings had grown.

Beers hated every document of the dirty little war, each an indictment of his imperial nation. Indeed, in Beers' firm judgment it had been nothing less than a racist crusade by white Cold Warriors employing a generous helping of Blacks as cannon fodder to kill little yellow men in a far off land. That might be a veritable quiver of cliches, but, by God! it was true.

Beers was himself "a World War II person" — so he

liked to tell his friends. Not only had the War set his life's course. It was much more than that.

World War II, he told his audiences, was "the last good war."

Why did he say this? He said it because his nation, having seen the total evil of fascism destroyed, had itself established an economic and military imperium, had succumbed to the hubris of global destiny, had yielded to an arrogance of power. It had backed right-wing dictators all over the world and suppressed the peoples' desire for democracy and equality at every juncture. The crime was stupendous, a serial of arrogance unending.

"But why do you stay with it, Lamm?" his academic friends asked, not fully aware of the handsome executive-level pay. "Why, you're part of the 'military-industrial complex' yourself." But they granted him "the last good war." Even his pacifist friends did that, perceiving to a man the totalitarian evil they believed unique to fascism.

The real trouble was that little of his work dealt any longer with that war. Almost exclusively, it was the Cold War and Vietnam that filled his project list. That was why, in recent years, he had spent more and more of his time at the Institute writing "last-good-war" reviews.

Beers cut short the tour and returned to his book-lined casemate. Numerous bright-jacketed books with flaming Messerschmidts, swastikas, and grinning faces of Ike crowded the shelves in double rows and files. From his desk he took up *Those Fabulous Girl Fliers of World War II* and began to read.

III

On the morning of the Monday Cheyenne was due to report, Beers pulled up in his neatly appointed Swedish car to observe an alien vehicle parked in his own reserved space. It was a red pickup truck, F O R D across the tailgate and two large bird dogs pacing the bed. There was a gun rack in the back window with guns in it! And it had Wyoming plates! In the next second, Beers was staggered by the most vicious bumper sticker he had ever seen:

When You're Hungry and Cold
And Sitting in the Dark,
Eat an Environmentalist

Beers felt as if his head was being seared simultaneously by flame and dry ice. Images of knives, guns and ropes twisted and flashed before him. Involuntarily, he stopped still, his head and upper body pointing intensely at the pickup. Puzzled, the pacing hounds tensed, uttering low growls.

He broke away, walking quickly to the Institute door, and burst in past the secretaries to slip down the vaulted corridor to his chamber in the bastion. Reaching it, he threw open the embrasure doors and leaned swaying into the breeze off the cool morning moat. Now he saw again the mother coot and her fledglings floating down the tide. Pleasant distinctive sounds came from high above him. Beers raised his head to see a wide V of mallards break formation and drop downward one by one to the refuge of the old fort.

"Duh-huck *blind!*" The shout, exploding behind him, almost sent Beers leaping through the embrasure. Shell-shocked, he swung around to see a tall figure in Levis emerge bent-headed from the arch. "Cheyenne," shouted the figure, gripping Beers' trembling hand in a muscular crush and running a gleaming eye down the vault to the embrasure. "But sure as hell, in here you'd need earplugs!" Rearing back on a long left leg, Cheyenne clapped the floor twice with his right boot sole, and the vault clapped back.

Another jolt followed.

Centered on Cheyenne's belt, Beers saw to his horror the bronzed figure of a beaten and bowed Native American! He almost cried out when he recognized the familiar art piece of the crude buckle symbol. It was the *End of the Trail!*

Rapid sharp footfalls sounded in the archway. A moment later, diminuitive Miss Washington assumed command of the room. The new arrivee's tour of the archives was now under way, she said. There were little flecks of foam on Beers' lips as he watched the new man exit, laughing, into the catacombs.

IV

A month passed. It was astonishing how fast Cheyenne "settled in," truly throwing himself into his book. Beers could not believe his good fortune after all — a second book author who could work unsupervised. Now he could devote nearly every afternoon to the reviews.

That is, if another problem had not come up that he soon found impossible to ignore.

One Sunday, Beers opened the books page of the newspaper to find not a Beers review, but a column by his new deputy, Damon. Its topic was the military industrial complex (!!) of the large socialist nation whose ideal, Beers, with important reservations, admired. Because of the untold suffering of that oft-invaded nation, he felt the point unfair. This unending paranoia that "the Russians are coming!"

When he took Damon to task the next day for this indiscretion, his deputy threw a Socratic dart that made his neck muscles tense. "Why did the military-industrial complex trouble Eisenhower the President," Damon wondered, waving to the laden shelves of the Normandy casemate. "When Eisenhower the General couldn't have landed without it?"

Beers had not previously pondered this Ike-ian dichotomy.

"Or perhaps, Lamm," said his deputy, leaning his packed bulk in Beers' direction while smiling, stroking his chin, and raising one eyebrow: "Perhaps Normandy was the 'last good' military-industrial complex?"

"What?!" Beers flinched sharply and could not muffle the shout. His face registered a stricken consternation. In the corridor, a staccato of steps sounded. Miss Washington appeared, forefinger to lips, glaring.

V

At three a.m. the honking from high above awakened Beers from the dream. Its vividness jolted him upright in bed.

"We abandoned them," said Damon, who stood before him dressed in a monks robe unaccountably of hunter orange. "They did not capitulate. *We* did."

"What?!" Beers had screamed.

"Have you forgotten the historic amendment?" Damon replied. "The tablet of peace from the moral mountaintop? 'No military action by this nation on the ground, or in the air, or off the shores of said lands.' But the moral demonstration didn't stop *their* flow of arms — not for one day."

"And the 'dominoes', " Damon continued. "They fell after all, didn't they? All along the Mekong. What is the symbol of our era? It is Cambodia."

Beers did not want to think about Cambodia. He drove from his mind that land and its scourges, the children of Marx, their leaders Sorbonne trained, who had emptied the cities and the villages in a vast death march to the forest camps, the sick, the weak and the aged and the very young dying all along the way. We shall erase all memory of the old, they had said, and they put a bullet in every educated brain. Two million had died in those terrible months. *That* was the domino, the bloodbath that many had said would come, and came with a vengeance. And Beers and his friends and the columnists they read said nothing in those years about the murder of the gentle land, until the holocaust could no longer be denied. Then, angered, they spoke out. "Politics!" they said in whispered fury.

"Politics!!" Beers spat out the word. On the other side of the bed, Beers' wife, Holly, stirred in her sleep.

"Politics? Oh, I see," said Damon of the dream. "Politics, not socialism."

"What is it, Lamm?" Holly mumbled sleepily. "Is it the hunters again?"

But it was not to end there, not to be a dream only, but the first in a sequence of dream and reality that came to him day and night with Damon. In his office and on the catacomb walks, they occurred each day. Yet he could not be sure that any one of them was real or whether, slumbering in his office chair, he had dreamed it. Nights, the intense exchanges woke him often, and he sat in his bed very cold and still.

At such times he felt as if he were a stone in a forest awaiting the event that would free it from its cold socket in the ancient earth and set in train its metamorphosis into some new unknowable thing or form.

Then, he was walking free in the forest, in the immaculate German forest, where they went under guard each evening to carry wood to the camp, where every tree rose in line, and no underbrush caught at his clothes, impeded his progress down the dim corridors of the forest.

The forest was deep and very dark. The corridor was endless, leading to no clearing. The dreams came as he walked, dreams of the dialogues in the casemate vaults or down the corridor's line of light. Damon was there always in the dreamy sequence of nighttime and day, of real and unreal. And when he sat at his desk he did not know whether the vision was substance or dream.

It became finally intolerable, and he resolved in the next dream or encounter, real or unreal, to destroy him. "Your kind are a memory! Dead!" he shouted. "The future will unfold on our terrain, not yours. The future of mankind is Man!" he shouted again. "And we will bury you in your little plots of holy ground."

"And what will 'Man' do with you, Beers?" the little monk, now clad fully in black, replied. "In the world you will, there is no place for you — for the individual. You will be buried in the same churchyard rubble — or just outside it. You are not quite 'socialist man,' Beers. *He* keeps no commandments of the heart — no 'moral law within me.' Even our deist Founder was in awe of the Law of Nature and Nature's God."

"Jefferson!" Beers shouted in exasperation. "Eighteenth century ideas! There is no God — of any kind. In the twentieth century, we have no need for any 'moral law within me.' That is all *crap* ! *Irrational crap* !"

"Yes, all 'crap'," Damon said. "Internal moral law is the difference between Jefferson and the architects of the holocausts of the twentieth century, those socialist and national socialist purifyings of the human race."

"How *dare* you!" he was shouting.

Rapid hard footfalls sounded nearby. Miss Washington appeared out of the caverns like a furious troll. In a quick glide, Beers moved out the arch and away, guns and knives gleaming and flashing in the leaping flames. In the corridor he surprised a research tour. Forty eyes shifted to record the face of a man whose features jerked violently side to side in repeated grotesque leers.

VI

The week at Okracoke was a godsend. Beers smiled at his own locution as he scanned the skies of the banks for feathered friends. Approaching down the strand, a group of "shellers" drew near, heads bent, eyes darting for the treasures of the tide. Beers, Holly, and other "birders" went by them, heads thrown back, eyes wide to the wonders of the air.

Okracoke, on the farthest Outer Banks, where you went by ferry, where no factory slug, no redneck, intruded. Okracoke was his restorative, and by the time they started home on Friday, it had washed his mind clean of the benighted crowd at the Institute. He was ready, anxious to return to his reviews and the last good war.

Saturday morning, he awoke at five preparing to read, but discovered he had left the fabulous girl fliers at the office the week before. Beers decided to drive in and retrieve the book before breakfast. Crossing the moat bridge, he observed the highest spring tide he had ever remembered seeing. It was lapping at the stone scarcely two feet below the first-tier embrasures.

Inside the fort, he turned into the street of the Institute, deserted except for a pickup truck at the far end. He pulled up beside the truck—Cheyenne's! Beers climbed out and walked alongside the vulgar conveyance. On the side window of the cab, a tiny rectangular decal caught his eye, and Beers stopped and bent to read it. What he there made out, in tiny letters, was that a prominent environmentalist organization, in which Beers held membership, "sucked".

He was trembling when he reached the door, which stood ajar. Beers stepped inside. At the far end of the dim, vaulted corridor, light shone out of the archway leading to his office. He reached the patch of light and, knees trembling, he moved unsteadily through the arch.

Far back in Beers' swivel, cleat boots gripping the desk edge, sat Cheyenne, his gleaming shotgun aimed out the open embrasure. Ear protectors like big saucers projected from his head. A big pointer, its back to Beers, faced the embrasure, trembling violently. Clasped tightly over its long, hanging ears were bright red earmuffs. To his horror Beers now heard through the embrasure the unmistakable call of a loon.

Two deafening blasts exploded in his ears, striking them so painfully that Beers instantly clapped his hands to his head. Cheyenne rocked forward through the smoke, as the pointer plunged through the embrasure and hit the moat legs churning.

"Get 'im! Get 'im, Boy!" Gun in hand, Cheyenne vaulted the desk, oblivious to the hot quaking object in the archway.

In seconds, the hound was leaping up out of the water, its muzzle clamped tight on the bloody kill. Squatting forward, Cheyenne pulled up through the wide opening the dripping dog and prize.

"Good boy!" he shouted, wresting the bird out of the pointer's mouth. The bill of the limp loon traced a thin red line across the floor. "Ain't she a beaut!" Cheyenne dropped to his knees to feel through the feathers where the pellets hit.

The hound, who had lost his earmuffs in the retrieval, stiffened as he detected the hot catatonic figure under the arch. With a low growl, he moved toward the stricken Beers. Excited and surprised, Cheyenne looked up, bloody bird in hand.

"Ain't she beautiful!" he shouted, holding forth the trophy. "Ain't she a beaut!"

"Oh, you dirty bloody fascist!!" the catatonic figure screamed, rocking on his heels. "You dirty fascist s—!"

VII

By the signed agreement, Cheyenne donated a full day's salary anonymously to the Wetlands Trust and stripped all environmentally offensive graffitti off his truck. In return, Beers did not fire his able assistant, nor did he file a complaint concerning the outrage. Cheyenne was not permitted to enter Beers' private office again for any reason. Communication was henceforth by written note.

Having scotched one tormentor, Beers determined now to go after the nemesis of his night and dreams, to subject the demon-monk to some utter and final humiliation and to break him. When he next saw Damon, he went for him in a white fury.

"We should form a team," he said, choking. "One . .

. me . . . representing enlightened liberalism. The other . . . you . . . reactionary paranoia!"

"*Enlightened* liberalism? A funny thing happened to
liberalism on the way to the future," the fat monk replied,
hooking a thumb in his tight girth-rope. "Why is it that
the more 'enlightened' liberalism becomes, the more it re-
sembles socialism?"

Beers struggled to reply, but already Damon was saying: "And why is justice a mockery in the socialist lands?
Why are there concentration camps wherever there is socialism?"

"Not *socialism* ," Beers shouted out. "You mean
Stalinism !"

"Can socialism endure without its Stalins?" Damon
said. "The 'Czech Spring' — what a brief season, like an
arctic summer. Can you really believe in the possibility of
'socialism with a human face'? Where has it ever existed?
Socialism excludes justice. It can't coexist with justice.
And tell me, Beers," continued his inquisitor. "Why does
every revolutionary commandante, sooner or later, go al-
tar-crawling to the Great Terrorist's tomb?"

Beers looked at his tormentor with unconcealed hatred. Here, more than mere bourgeois pap, was an arrant,
arrogant questioning of History itself.

How did one answer insolence so invincible?

Lamm Beers did not call himself a socialist. But he
knew that the politics he professed could no longer be recognized as liberalism and that Damon was surely right.
"Votaries of liberty" — that, liberals no longer were. Not
with the unfinished agenda. Not in this criminally un-

equal North-South world of very rich and very poor. That, and not the residual brutalities from Russia's Old Regime, was the reality of the declining century. Socialism—how had the Berkeley students said it? Socialism is the End of History.

He came out of his reverie with the wild apprehension that the little priest had penetrated his thoughts.

"Socialism," said Damon, "is *le neant* . It is the End of Man."

"What do you mean?" Beers said quickly.

"It is the commanding fact of our time," Damon said. "Not overpopulation, not the 'North-South dialogue', not 'the environment', or declining energy resources — none of these. *Socialism* is the dark star our world is approaching. *It* is the force that will or will not determine man's future for the next epoch."

"What do you mean?" Beers asked again. "Socialism is nothing more than economics — than economic justice!"

"No, socialism is not only economic dogma," Damon said. "It is something profoundly different. No, no, it isn't just the business of abolishing private property and ownership. If it were only that, then why the implacable hatred of socialism for religion? Why the attack on the family, which you find everywhere in socialist literature — read *The Communist Manifesto* . And all the socialist states try to impose this holy trinity of 'anti'. Can that be explained on economic grounds? No, socialism is not just a failed economic dogma. It is an ideology embracing every part of human existence in its death grip."

"And is that why socialism is so popular with twenty-year-olds at your Sorbonne — death?" But Beers' voice quaked as he spoke the word he never used. His legs felt very heavy, and he slumped into a carrel chair.

"Yes, that's why."

"Yes?!"

"Death beckons to every social revolutionary: 'Come, die for me.' Death. The Russian nihilists enshrined it. Bakunin too. And in our own time, Baader-Meinhof and the Red Brigades. 'All together we shall die.' The death wish is the motive force of socialism. Socialism is Thanatos. Socialism is the death instinct."

The blood dream. Blood and bodies in the jungle camp. The reality pursued him as a dream, the death laager on the Caribbean rim, the vats of red death, the thousand bodies, black and white, men, women, little children lying in the jungle sun.

"It's simple, it's simple," the handsome leader said. "There is nothing to cry about. We should rejoice. We have lived as no other people have lived. No, no hysterics now. We are socialist people. Let us go now. No more, no more. No, no fear, we will die. Hurry, my children, hurry. Quickly, quickly, quickly, quickly. All together we shall die."

He was walking down the corridor of the dark forest. But it was no longer the immaculate German forest. Wild strange plants grew into the path, and he had to push them aside to make his way.

The corridor was lightening, the trees no longer distinct or tall, but dwarfing sharply. He found himself in an undifferentiated maze of thickening, twisting undergrowth. He pushed on slowly. The tangled plants, waist high, spread to the horizon in a dense uniform plane of green.

Still, he made his way through, though it seemed that the tangle resisted, caught at his clothes. But the light grew brighter, a reflecting light, not suffusing, but bright and cold as if artificial, and as he continued his way, it illuminated without depth or shade the plane of stunted limbs and twisted undergrowth.

He became aware of an approaching coldness. But he moved farther along, drawn to the light. To either side now, the plants appeared shrunken in a tangle of gray. The light grew brighter. He could no longer distinguish the path, and he raised his eyes from the blinding ambience.

Before him rose the great glass Titan, the shining form of heroic Man, eternal, towering to the sky, its features perfect, pure, and he cried out with joy and stretched his arms upward to the Shining Titan.

A tinkling sound rose on the wind. It multiplied into the clashing of a thousand tinkling sounds, splintering, shattering the light. Ice-like splinters fell around him, needles, and great shards. The light declined rapidly. It grew very cold. An icy black night descended. Beers stood shivering alone in the void, waiting.

ZARATHUSTRA

The law is broken; nature is disobeyed;
and the rebellious are outlawed, cast forth,
and exiled, from this world of reason, and
order, and peace, and virtue, and fruitful
penitence, into the antagonist world of
madness, discord, vice, confusion, and
unavailing sorrow.

— *Edmund Burke*

I

It was said that Brennen held seances and that that was why the leading novelist of the decade was something of a recluse. Brennen had in fact taken to table an apostate bishop seeking contact with his suicide son. But as with nearly everything you heard about Brennen, the outcome remained conjecture. The bishop died dehydrated in a mystic's cave above the Dead Sea, no further light shed. Brennen was known, as the jacket blurbs said, almost exclusively through his writing.

Was it that guardedness, that insistence on both celebrity and privacy granted no one else that would bring Peter Roan that fall to the festival at Montran, the "Year of Brennen"? That was my first thought about the season's announced enfant terrible. But Roan, I would learn, was a different riddle altogether in the mystery surrounding the enigmatic Michael Brennen.

Roan had just published an intellectual sensation. Out of Vanderbilt or Virginia — "some Southern nowhere," so it was sounded from our high citadel — Peter Roan had come with "Zarathustra's Return."

The Roan essay was an audacious moral turnaround, at midpoint, of Nietzsche's great doom prophecy of the "ruin" of Christian morality—"that great spectacle in a hundred acts which is reserved for the next two centuries." From his late-twentieth century vantage, Zarathustra looked down with horror across the blood-pools of a darkling plain to the rising bulk of an immense high massif, black and smoking against a burning sky. Below the burning peaks, protruding cliffs of bones flickered in the red light. Blood streams ran down the massif into black pools which magnified the immense and horrific structure blocking the horizon.

The burning blood massif was the accumulation of all the martyred humanity of the holocaust century. But beyond the peaks, Zarathustra espied the infinitely more terrifying horrorscape of the final age, a "hideous epoch" of abounding cataclysm and the final descent of man ungoverned by any remnant of moral law.

But Roan's Zarathustra, stunned by the terrible vision, recoiled from the prophecy, now half elapsed, to describe an alternative vision. Zarathustra declared a "taking back" of the secular patrimony, a stopping and reversal of the revaluation of values which Nietzsche had seen and welcomed but which, in its elimination of a universal morality, had opened the way to the killing by the state of whole classes and peoples in the gulags and Sobibors of the totalitarian century.

"Zarathustra Returns" was a revolutionary tract whose speaker recalled his master's beginning doubts, before the darkness set in, about the great destruction he had wrought and his vain attempt to go beyond it: "I want to learn to be human again." Zarathustra-in-return, recoiling before the hemorraging structures of civility and sanity, with great emotion and beauty of expression viewed the deep world with new eyes.

The Zarathustra of Peter Roan drew terrifying pictures of the pending civilizational collapse, dramatized its causes, noted that the destruction proceeded from an amputated intellectual framework that did not fit human nature. If the evidence of the epochal crisis was clear, so too was the way out: the recognition that man's nature was spiritual. Zarathustra, with great intellectual force and with a beauty of language that continued the lyrical ride of one hundred years ago, declared a new day, a new *ja-sagende* epoch seated in a rebirth of religious consciousness.

The cultural organs had rejected summarily "ZR", but it was seized upon and published in the summer by the most influential of the rising new journals. Almost immediately reprinted by avid promoters, it spread by internet to friend and foe to sweep and stun its readers, delighting admirers while placing in outraged deshabille the leading priestly class.

It was with this calling card that Roan announced his coming, uninvited, to the literary festival at Montran, organized to celebrate the Brennen oeuvre. It was said in many places that the Nobel would one day come to Brennen, and the citadel's promotion was an effort to that end. Nor did Brennen play recluse to his reputation. His promise to participate drew to the festival nationwide literary excitement. Alone, the return of the recluse promised to make

Montran the event of the season. "ZR's" treasonous obtrusion? For that, the Method would suffice: the unsaid silence by which insolence is answered. But the citadel had not reckoned with a Zarathustra in the flesh.

"Zarathustra Returns" was without question a direct assault on Brennen's whole "thrust." Of all contemporary novelists, none, his critics said, had advanced the novel of the absurd farther toward autodestruction. His purpose was the obliteration of meaning. In his stories, mock quests led nowhere. Love, identity, science, art, language existed as a fantastic game with no rules. His method was to dislocate time, space, and all causality.

Brennen was indeed on the record that his literary mission was nothing less than "a revolution in the consciousness of our time." Brennen's metaphors of violence and absurdity depicted a spent universe moving toward destruction, and a recast human nature fitted to that new memoryless and chaotic age. Death, excrement, animalistic powers, madness, were his metaphors. Brennen did not believe that there was a hole the size of God in every man. He believed only in the hole.

II

Brennen the recluse — but I had known him before the absurdist novels and the rise and the Pulitzer, before the Return of Zarathustra.

I had met Michael Brennen on a ship to Rotterdam, the only other American at the table. We were both bound for Heidelberg, I discovered — I on a German A.K.T.A.

scholarship that won me Petra that year, he to study, he'd drolly said, the "paradigm of the American police state." Brennen was no juvenile, his quest was serious: the riven land, the dichotomous culture in whose breast, as every German knows, two hearts fervently beat. Germany, land of dualities: what would the Germanies, and old Europe, teach Michael Brennen, poet, brightest of eye, literary priest-to-be, child of our times?

Our interests were dissimilar — my passion was the German *Romantik* and my visions the clerestories and choirs of the high medieval. Still, I saw him often during his Heidelberg stay. He was reading all the great builders and destroyers — Kant and Rousseau, Hegel, Nietzsche, Marx, and Freud.

He was also working through his earliest stories — tales even the first of which hinted ambivalently at our century's loosed moorings. When I read these disturbing and penetrating inquiries, in some warm Gasthaus or cafe, with Brennen sitting by gazing into the mid-distance where hovered some new, strangely shadowed vision, I had a presentiment of the nay-saying genius in the forming.

Brennen had joined one of the young socialist fellowship groups of those halcyon nonviolent days before Berkeley and Vietnam, before Baader-Meinhof. Synthesis beckoned in these innocent groups, and one day we joined an overflow crowd in the alte Aula to hear one of our travelling countrymen, a bright Harvard spirit, declare to thunderous applause: "We are all liberals. We are all conservatives. We are all socialists." Little did we know.

Brennen was also learning to box, though slender in build—a young writer's impulse that paralleled a subtle pugnacity I began to notice in his stories. But it was the boxing that produced the incident that ended his Heidelberg stay toward the close of the year and that, I was to learn, sealed for life my friendship with Michael Brennen, archangel of destruction.

It started in a Gasthaus on the Neckar at the foot of the steep cobbled rise to the Old Bridge, one of those historic inns where a dueling fraternity came weekly in their bright sashes and caps to drink at tables where Goethe had dined and Jean Paul composed.

I had just met Petra, and we were sitting at a lively table where a great boot of beer went round and round to huzzahs and shouts and wild student songs. All of the sudden, I noticed Brennen across the room, seated half facing away at Jean Paul's table, where he was emptying a large stein. I was just about to call out to him when the small drama in which he had become involved made me hesitate.

Brennen was staring with no hint of human warmth at a huge ox of a student at the next table whose dueling scar was so fresh and livid I guessed the bandage must have come off that very day. There were other new scars there, too. The year was well along—nearly every young duellist had acquired his social mark. Brennen's duellist of the eye stolidly returned the unfriendly stare: "two beer-soaked brains in ocular deadlock," Brennen put it later, during his recovery. Both tables at length fell silent, and soon the entire room grew quiet.

It was just at the "pin drop" moment that Brennen, pugnaciously drunk, inquired of the student why was it the Burschenschaft boys were all cut up: was it menstruation envy, or Nazi puberty rites?

They took care to bear him through the door before they started beating him. But the respect paid to Goethe's inn was fatal for the ox. As he went through the doorway, Brennen had just time to land two sharp jabs square on the scar that tore it wide open. In the street, they fell savagely on him with fist and boot, beating him almost unconscious. When I managed to push through to the street, they were dragging him through the portcullis, and as I reached the bridge they heaved him over into the Neckar. The police were on the way, but I am certain to this day that Brennen, his shoulder broken, would have drowned if I had not gone in and brought him out of the river.

Later that year on a back street, I saw the ox, the pretty duelling crescent now an ugly streetfighters scar.

Brennen's broken shoulder took some time to heal. But he continued his great destroyers regimen in bed, completing all of Rousseau, stoically suffering Marx for two weeks, and actually reading Freud. But it was the lyric of Nietzsche that he took as scriptural text and song of songs. With this heavy-light baggage, Brennen left for Paris in the spring, soon after he got out of the hospital — all according to plan, he said, but he'd also heard that the ox was laying for him.

It was in Paris that Brennen would begin the great dense and difficult nay-saying novels so utterly of the Zeitgeist, that made him famous. Paris: womb claimant of

American writers, self-styled progenitor of all sensibility in those uniform years of existence cum marxisme.

His novels would fall on eager ears, those dense and fantastic tales in which mockery sat laughing in every chamber of an aimless sphere spinning in the random void. But in the succession of tales told, there grew on an unflinching hardness, and a sense of a temblor shift of vast substructures whose direction was disintegration. Everywhere in his writing, Brennen bore witness to a civilization no longer under moral control, to a world whose pilgrims viewed all vanishing bonds and institutions as mocking deceptions, to a world utterly material, whose rock of ages was transmuted to a lava stream running in all directions into an icy sea.

But the life of the maturing novelist was to lie outside my observation. After exchanging a few faithful letters, each more hurried and tardy than the last, we lost touch. In the meantime, my studies were drawing to an end. The year after Brennen left Heidelberg I completed the last phase of my art studies and returned with my new wife to California.

I did see Brennen once more before we left. It was by chance and it was in Basel, where Petra and I had gone on a brief trip from Heidelberg. Brennen was spending there a few weeks' on-site invocation of the tortured spirit of Friedrich Nietzsche, Professor of Classical Philology, 1869-1879.

I surprised the figure so familiar to me at the Erasmus tomb in the Munster, where he stood studying closely the Latin inscription honoring the great humanist, votary of the Middle Way. Hearing my footstep, Brennen turned, the hardness new in his expression giving way to a familiar reserved friendliness as he spied his tavern-mate.

As we talked about his writing and the tyrannies of the Left Bank, which he did not think were tyrannies, and of my marriage and pending departure, we walked out of the cathedral onto the wide high porch above the Rhine. Basel — on the Rhine's medieval highroad, heart of the Christian West — once, with its humanists, the "Left Bank" of Europe. But Brennen had come not to Erasmus' Basel, or to Burckhardt's — that Renaissance scholar without equal — but to Nietzsche's. And he had come on a linear pilgrimage whose direction was no longer in doubt. For Michael Brennen, amoral tribune, the universe denied to its farthest atom any remnant "middle way," knew inevitabilities only, knew and required the running out of the spiritual and the end of the ages' great myth.

"The long-dying God," Brennen said as we stood before Erasmus' gray fortress in Nietzsche's city. "He will not need another hundred years. It is I who shall finish Him!"

From their window on the Rhine and the West, the Swiss watched, in the century's second decade, the shattering of Europe's ordered structures; watched, in its third and fourth decades, the collapse of the European world into the totalitarianisms and holocausts of the God-alien men, the *terribles simplificateurs* whose coming Basel's Burckhardt had foretold.

III

Brennen, Brennen, burning those twenty years that saw our century go from its respite of confident hope into the time of troubles in which we would live, liberated from the moral canopy of the past, liberated from ourselves. Brennen, Brennen, burning bright, fey archangel of the night.

I became the teacher of art history I had in Heidelberg wished to be. With Petra I came to California, to literature's high citadel where I play my modest supporting role to the workshops of writing. My students, historyless savages, call my classes their "nostalgia trip," not relevant in the high dells of deconstruction where they flounder, studying beauty in filth and art in dementia. But I teach them the endurance of harmony.

Was it fortuitous that I found myself after seven years again in the proximity, though not the company, of Michael Brennen? With his fabled success had come independence and the reclusiveness he demanded and that would rule the remainder of his life. Brennen bought as a recluse haven a tract in the mountains southward down the coast from Montran, a five-hour trip from the city by a precarious private road. On his remote site high over the ocean, he constructed a mountain eyrie which had — so it was said in the ironic "end-time" idiom of the citadel — the final view of the sinking Western sun.

But Brennen spent few of the intervening years in his California eyrie. He was a recluse, not a hermit, and he found much of the day-to-day anonymity he wanted on

the Continent, where his dense works, translating poor-
ly, were less well known. And he encountered in Europe
fewer young predators trying for the coup, literary or sexual—his way was freer there as he travelled, the cultural
terrorist, incognito from haven to haven.

Was Brennen wishing anonymity now, I wondered, for
"Who was Peter Roan?" was the question on every quiver-
ing lip of our clerisy. On the eve of the Brennen celebration,
Roan remained as much a mystery figure as he had been
during the summer's lightning strike of "Zarathustra's
Return". No entry in the directories of national scholars or
in any Who's Who, not even in the one for the South and
the Southwest. Nothing at all anywhere of the seditious
scholar of insidious insight.

A very young man, perhaps? But what young man is
old, as Zarathustra is old? The Nietzsche specialists of-
fered no help either; these scholars were as incensed as
the cultural celebrities and high priests. A European? The
speculation so far had led nowhere. Roan's appearing was
indeed "the WASP in the woodpile" — I borrow yet another locution of the citadel.

The Year of Brennen drew on, a week's succession of
exhibitions and occasions to culminate in the Reading, by
the Master, in the Greek Theater. Monday of the week, Petra
and I went to see the spectacular Rory Danneman exhibition, which was touted as the first post-mortem showing
of the striking black-white Danneman photo images—the
naked mountain domes, shimmering tree arbors, the lava-
like rivers flowing in the sun. At Danneman's death, the

news anchors had all shown zoom-ins of their personal favorites.

The exhibit's title had been adapted from the famous "Moon Rising" photograph. "Who Can Create a Moonrise?" we read, as we entered the gallery. We passed a desk manned by a pale and bony manikin. In her severe black dress and black cockaded cap, an apparent mourner's headdress, she struck me as the image of a nun of art.

It was at this point that my wife violated the intended sanctity of the Danneman enshrinement.

"Only God, can create a moonrise," Petra said.

I do not know why the nun put herself through a disbelief routine so painstaking — it was lost on my wife. Respecting highly the derivative creativity of Danneman's exceptional camera eye, she had already moved along to an intent study of the collection.

As I looked at Danneman's photo studies, I was struck as I had often been by their static quality. It was a quality reinforced by the almost absolute clarity that Danneman often achieved. Perhaps this was why our urbanized culture, which styled nature environment, marvelled in a kind of uncritical mass gape at Danneman's depiction of natural wonder viewed without distraction through clear air. But his great gift — much more than the brilliant client insight that had made him wealthy — was his understanding of light, not for nothing the Christian metaphor.

Danneman knew the subordination of all things to light, that the universe consisted not of its great void, but of its light, and that light was all. To this insight, he added the gift of patient waiting for the moment when light created majestic beauty.

Yet the static quality of Danneman's superb vision was impossible to pass over. In his world of wonder, there were no animate things, no human beings. His communion with nature was not a shared communion. The majestic chasms and great ranges of light were his alone, unsullied by any human figure, any reminder of an inhabited earth. It did not surprise me that when Danneman died, his material exit was rigorously in the Eastern mode: cremation, no urn, no stone, no memory, a scattering far out to sea, and nothingness.

"There is a hole in his pictures the size of man," Petra said at the turnstiles — her inimitable way of putting a cap on things. Now, the nun could only gape.

That night we went to the chapel-studio of Emil Degen, an occasion of literary spectacle — an opportunity, too, to see the recent pieces of the citadel's permanent sculptor in residence.

Degen purportedly was Brennen's eminence grise, but that was an exaggeration, given Brennen's extended European wanderings. Still, there was an established bond between them. Degen's dissevered torsos, heads, and limbs had several years ago launched the Disintegration School. Disintegration had become all the rage in the galleries, driving out the canvases of light and all survivals of the complete human form. Scaled for living room utility, Degen's provocative torsos — straining brasses and trunks of opulently textured plastic that writhed in orgasm and death — carried the "little death" metaphor to the shocking extreme. His individualized severed heads, alive still, looked out on their disembodied state in grimaces of grostesque self-mockery. The Degen Heads were regarded as "hilarious" by their owners.

Degen came, I knew, out of the German "Stunde Null" generation that had come of age at the very point of the "caesura" of 1945. Degen's own caesura theory was extreme. History had — with Auschwitz, Hiroshima, and the German firestorms — ceased to obtain. Nineteen forty-five: Hour Zero, nothing beside remains, the Apocalypse is begun, let us shovel out the debris.

Degen had met his prophet in Paris in 1968 and had followed Brennen to his Montran eyrie the next year. He had paid court assiduously, I'd heard, and became Brennen's agent at the citadel: the ultimate disciple. He also came to look after some of his publishing — Degen's contacts were unrivalled. The Brennen editions were well done, the Brennen mystique sculpted by devoted hands.

Degen's own artistic unfolding progressed meantime. He was a minor cult figure, too, and drew to himself a changing coterie, a bisexual troupe of student actors and artists with whom he staffed, in the nude, his shocking exhibitions. Degen took his toll of those who beat about his flame, for he made films of very high quality of his dewy young proteges, for selected viewings.

I had been to Degen's chapel twice before. I had gone once to photograph, with permission, the stained glass, which was brilliant and fine. Degen's studio gallery was a model of the Gothic, scale small but structuring true, built before the First World War by old money, employing Italian artisans, in the service of Episcopalian tastes.

The glass was not European, but American. Its creator had drawn on a capitalist fortune to produce glass for his clients of richest brilliance, using the powder of ground-up gems as an admixture and sometimes working whole stones into the religious figuration.

Degen had acquired his church long after the estate it was attached to had disappeared. The house had served a declining succession of inhabitants down to a radical writers colony that had burned it to the ground during a riotous hand-to-hand over the Hitler-Stalin Pact in 1939. Degen's own depredations upon the estate's surviving Gothic annex had been severe. Though he'd spared the glass for its brilliance, he had had all the inscription and bas-relief painstakingly chiseled away within and without.

On that visit, I had surprised Degen without his mask, the dark glasses he wore always outside his studio. I shall never forget his naked eyes, deepset and frightening, sooty beards beneath, a pornographer's eyes, and Degen took pains to conceal in that intelligent face the animalism that shone in them, as I have seen in the eyes of beasts, waiting and wary. Degen studied with irritation the involuntary revulsion I registered, and tore his sunglasses furiously from his pocket to mask those desolated windows.

I had paid another visit to the chapel during the decade of protest, when Montran's art colony had risen to the challenge of the "unspeakable" war. "Days of Rage" solicited not high art so much as spontaneity, and Degen had assembled an exhibition of unforgettable canvases and cartoons.

In one rendering, Liberty held aloft a torch of rockets and bombs. In another, helmeted Nazis bayoneted yellow-skinned children while maintaining gigantic Red White and Blue erections. In a third, the President grinned hideously from behind a mountain of skulls — his personal handiwork, the artist meant subtlely to say. Afterwards, the artists of Montran had arranged their works into a giant collage, which was printed as a full-page antiwar statement with 175 signatures appended.

Thus, Degen's chapel, well-worn stage for the inventive mockeries of the festival of Brennen. Here, Nietzsche's prophecy was long since realized. With Petra, I entered upon Degen's profane occasion without any illusion.

The first thing visible as we went in was one of my girl students naked and recumbent on a bed-like bier as one-half of an exhibition entitled "Joy of Androgny." My student and the male androgyne lay in quiet but unquestionably joined embrace, my student on top, the shaven heads, silver earrings and cosmetics concealing not at all the truer nature of the joy. I could not imagine that this still life would hold for long.

Coming down the center of the nave was a figure in the full white regalia of the Bishop of Rome. As he passed, the crowd gave way, tittering as blessings were received. Administered with single uplifted finger, these were sounded in a sing-song litany composed inventively of the Anglo-Saxon four-letter ten, in gerunds.

The pope passed by, and I looked upward to the clerestory and the untouched glass. But Degen had covered it over with great banners, which announced the gala's theme: D I S O R I E N T A T I O N

Book figures ambled and danced through the crowd. Of the Cheerybles, Degen had made a pair of merry gays, and of Scarlett O'Hara a gushing black belle. Ivan Denisovich was there in gulag rags — and a Native American head-dress.

Degen had placed his new sculptures in the transepts. One of the pieces was the already favorably reviewed "Jack Bites the Dust." This piece of aggravated black humor was a brightly painted plaster depiction of the assassination scene at the very moment of death. Degen had frozen the figures in the convertible into catatonic attitudes, render-ing the faces ugly masks of rage. Precisely that — to add to death, rage, and to take delight in the victim's death-rage — was the Degen gift — *Schadenfreude* , as the Germans said, and with a vengeance.

Eerie, shifting light — reddish, then a paling green, and black light dense and heavy — altered constantly the kalei-doscopic scene. The boundless profanity of rock echoed up and down the sacred stone. Mendocino Fine was ubiq-uitous through the place, and they were taking cocaine at the batismal font. We were just checking out the sights in the choir — a drag queen in the garb of a Carmelite nun stays in memory — when at the far end of the church a cho-rus of cheers arose pierced by oles, whistles, and shrieks. The joy of androgyny had climaxed.

But an episode still more bizarre was yet to come. The music died away as a solemn line of leather-clad women filed into the chapel, forming up in two facing lines down the center of the nave. There were sixty or seventy of them, of all ages. Some were bare-breasted, but all were dressed in gray, green, or brown jerkin affairs, which made some of the younger ones resemble out of humor wood nymphs.

The stern change produced a crowd oddly subdued, given the available sights thus far. At a prearranged signal, the women began individually to pick different vocal notes, which they held, catching their breaths at different times, so that an eerie, unmodulated drone filled the chapel that continued unabated for some time. The weird dirge must have gone on ten or twelve minutes until the women one by one fell silent.

A tall bony figure strode forward to interpret the symbolic event. That which we had just witnessed, said Jade of the Mountain, spoke to the burgeoning spiritual dimension of the Movement. Some of the women were witches, she explained — though not all.

Degen's Disorientation banner came loose just at that moment from the high wall, falling like a shroud upon the crowd opposite us. For a few moments, the banner leaped and heaved in a frenzy of hidden action. I turned to see Degen, standing apart from the crowd, watching the leaping shroud with an odd intensity. Then, with a shout, the revellers threw off the banner and stepped free.

But the wood-witch dirge had placed a damper on Degen's occasion that he had surely failed to foresee. The chapel began now to empty of Cheerybles, androgynes, literati mind-blown, and unshockable teachers of art history with wives. At the door, we stopped to let the last lost celebrants pass into the night as the chapel went dark. Through the high clerestory the bright moon illuminated the brilliant glass — tapestry of the Christian centuries with all their reserves of mercy and forgiveness.

IV

The change in Michael Brennen was striking. I met him just as he came out of the complex of the upper campus trailing a bustling celebrity's crowd. There were cameramen running, breathless student girls, excited bearded men in hornrims, hurrying. But Brennen, Degen tagging by his side, walked as if alone, the plaza crowd yielding before him as to a Prussian field marshal, or a holy man.

His hair was shoulder-length, and completely white — an exact complement to his black close-fitting European dress, a scholars garb from the last century. He wore over his shoulders a long black coat, which hung on him like a cape. Brennen at forty had still the slimness of youth, but he walked now with a grace of movement new to my observation, his step silent and firm. More striking than in my remembrance was the intense seriousness of his features, and he had, undimmed, that brightest of eye that I had ever looked into.

And his eye met mine, and he nodded imperceptibly and smiled lightly as he moved on and down the long stone incline of the plaza like an incarnation of the poet Stefan George in old Heidelberg of eighty years ago. I turned to watch him disappear into the entrance of the great dolmen that was the high keep of the citadel, Brennen, poet-voice of the era whose seas are rising, they are heaving.

Then in my reverie, I remembered suddenly the fleeting glimpse of Degen bustling angrily by. From that desperate face the mask was gone, the eyes burning coals. And at the doorway to the dolmen, the disciple was shouting.

The crowd turned now to the morning entertainments in the Greek Theater that lay just under the dolmen shadow, and in some confusion I drifted with the crowd, not able to absorb my encounter, after twenty years, with Michael Brennen. But now, sounds came from the dais that momentarily drove away the vision of Brennen. I looked up to see Freund, one of the citadel's middle-aged exotics, "bathing" the young student crowd in the cadenced obscenities for which he enjoyed some reputation. The "bathing" had been Freund's method during the war. Thus had he dehumanized our political leaders who, he said, were f — — — the bleeding wombs of Southeast Asia. A corporation, I heard him say now, was like a gigantic a — — —, and the ranches and the villas of the rich were the places they built to s — in. Thus far Freund, doctor of literature, teacher of youth, warming up the crowd.

Freund had shifted gears. He was describing now the hope of history as it would be realized in the authentic, communal, caring nations of the dream. In those lands, Freund related, they were dispossessing all the feudal forces, and that included the Church, and from the dream there would emerge one day a truly human community. But these remarks were only a prelude to more colorful entertainment. Latin rhythms began to sound out of the theater wings.

Several students came onto the central dais, all light skinned, but wearing Hispanic worker ensembles. That they had cut sugarcane for the Revolution seemed to be the main point of this sequence. Among the anglo Latins stood a beautiful dark-haired girl wearing an incongruous headband and feather and a very short leather skirt. In the distance, a bongo drummer in the lower plaza took up his mid-morning routine.

Still other feathered men and women waited their turn on the stone benches — the rally's next phase. Then, with a clenched-fist salute and a battle shout in incomprehensible Spanish, the vicarious Venceremos departed the stage in all directions, leaving the feather girl, swaying slightly, alone on the dais.

She was there to introduce the Actor, and she did this neither gutturally nor in Latin sing-song but in good general American — though somewhat incoherently.

In transition from middle age to old, Candallion had grown more than moderately stout. Completely done out in beaded leather, he rolled onto the stage with efficient quickness. The movie idol referred to himself as "Sixkiller". The girl was June Little Feather. She was half Hispanic, one quarter-blooded Native American, and one-eighth White Rapist, Sixkiller said.

Candallion launched into one of those astonishing analogies in which the Trail of Tears and the trains to Auschwitz coalesce as a Founding Fathers' belated surprise, but no one was listening. The whole theater was

watching June Little Feather, who was swaying to a different drummer altogether— the bongo man, whose rhythms
had grown more insistent and nearer. On the high wing
and soaring, Little Feather had gone into an explicitly sexual routine, her skirtlet bouncing to reveal pantyless loins.
The drumming grew louder, increasing. Black Caribbeans
snake-danced into the Greek Theater, drowning out
Sixkiller in the encompassing calypso, and that was it for
the sins of Custer.

The sessions that week had been the usual micro-
scopic treatments with quibbling critique, but a group of
Brennen's student admirers ignored the laboratory format
in favor of pure readings of selections from the oeuvre in
a large hall.

Once again the Brennen bombast, furious tornadic
action dissipating, directionless. Forays down dark light-
ning-seared ways to ineluctable dead ends, gentility and
violence in brilliant, shocking juxtaposition, the melding
of evil and good. In the readings, the sun rose golden to
explode into an eternal nuclear darkness. Phantoms boldly stalked the lighted ways. In the glass of Chartres, evil
grinned from hidden patterns in the faces of the saints.

The mockery of Christian symbology was severe, as
shocking as when I had read Brennen's first Paris pieces.
Who now could walk in innocence through the Notre Dame
and not imagine the anti-God grinning, the evil resident in
all beauty? These were images stunning still, but I could
not bear them today. They were now to me corrosive and
alien, no longer softened in their tinctures by memory of
the friend of my youth. I left the hall where ruled the gods

of disorientation, and I walked outside along the terraces, past the eucalyptus groves to the cluster of the rising redwoods, and I thought about the Return of Zarathustra and the continuing mystery of Peter Roan.

By late week, Roan had not, as promised, appeared. Would he arrive on Brennen's final day?

Brennen's hour was three, in the Greek Theater. I went early to get a seat close in, but the ampitheater was already nearly full when I arrived, and I had to find a place high in the back in the eucalyptus' shadow, where I shivered in the cool dry air.

Round about the rising discs of the dais, I could see, even from my vantage, the magnitude of the literary array, a differentiated and bizarre spectacle of the literary physiognomy, the atomized treasonous clerks of letters, alienation's communicants, creedists of the profane almost to the last despiritualized soul — art's alien nation.

Over the theater loomed the slitted dolmen that housed the highest citadel. I glanced up at the busy warren with its hungry eyes, a barren laboratory where humanity was studied amputated of its history, like a species of deep-sea fish newly discovered, about which nothing is known and all the questions remain to be asked. In the dolmen, interdiscipline ruled, historyless. Degen had there a high loft and sculpted aggression-free South Sea nudes to whom he gave a certain mocking air. I went seldom to the dolmen warren, and when I did, felt always hunted.

At least half a dozen camera crews were crowding the foot of the stage. They blocked views, drawing from the sitting congress of sensibility, angry obscenities. The networks were there, not missing a decadent beat, attentive ever to the ritual in its unending refinement, following like ever tinier spiders the running out of order in the far-spun threads of art autonomous.

Brennen emerged suddenly, black-clad, from the wings, white hair streaming, Mephistopheles striding the stage—I could not help it. Then, he began to speak, the words dense and precise, the images stunning as I remembered from the conversations of our youth.

And in all the crowd of thousands, his eyes sought out mine and it was to me, high in the shadow, that he spoke, face uplifted, out of the West and the world on the flood-tide of the rising sea.

And he spoke to me, each word a shining incandescence brightening and deepening the firmament in its fullness. Then, from the marble bowl of brilliant light, I saw the tiny red flash high in the dolmen with its slits of eyes, and within his great black cape-coat, Michael Brennen—Peter Roan—collapsed lifeless onto the dais of Montran.

V

They caught Degen in the warren lot just short of his car, his weapon cased, but he died a day later from a capsule he swallowed in his cell. The archives, by Brennen's instruction, came to me, and the whole testament whose foreword in the Greek Theater had signalled its contents, the rosy dawn of Zarathustra in Return, the taking back of the nighmare epoch that lay beyond the holocausts, the

Great Recalling of the Destroying Fathers, and the return of Michael Brennen to the rejoicing coasts of light.

Here is the story of the Return of Zarathustra that I now publish to a stunned world, the torn, triumphant odyssey of Michael Brennen, pilgrimage of modern man, the seeing through, in the deep world, to the firmament of light.

———

The war: it was not as the Interpreters said — burning the villages and killing the children. Who will dispute the hideousness of war, devourer of man? Yet, we did not burn and kill by policy in cold blood. Ask the Interpreters now of the victory of the dream-men, and of policy, and cold blood.

Why did we make the war? To stop the creeping-on of the century's lethal dream.

Here is my sleep-thief: There is a ravine in a cold and sodden woods that is dry and warm, and people are sheltering in the ravine. The people are happy and laughing. Then, a great gray shroud drops over them. Dagger-men run quickly out of the dark woods and under the shroud, and the gray cloth begins to leap and to heave with their efficient, quick violence. They work quickly and are gone, the dagger-men of the dream.

But my sleep-thief does not leave me, for there is another sheltering ravine where the people are waiting and are happy and laughing. And a gray shroud falls over them, and the dagger-men work quickly and are gone. And one by one the sheltering places of the happy people are made blood-pits, and happiness and hope are gone from the land.

It is almost beyond comprehension that I, and so many of my generation, viewed the dream exclusive of its blood-history. It was not that that history was unrecorded and lost. In spite of all the attempts in the lands of power to veil the killings, they are the terrible stained document of the twentieth century.

My countrymen were not themselves of the dream, yet they acclaimed its creeping-on, holding freedom to be an accident of history — a bourgeois bubble as certain to disappear as the fealty oath. They did not ask those peoples under the dream what their wish was, nor did they know them or ask to know them, but they spoke freely for them. And they took as their talisman a hatred of their own.

It was what lay beyond and animated the order we possessed that they could not abide, because it existed above them. They could not live in its light, which overshone their own guttering flame. And so they sought to shroud the world from the light. They sought the night.

And when the war was lost, the night that they willed descended on those peoples. In the gentlest land, where the people were beautiful and small, the cadres of the dream brought down the darkest night. And the killing began again, the closing of the hospitals and the schools, the markets and the homes, the emptying of the cities in a vast jungleward migration. And they died by the thousands and the tens of thousands all along the way. The cadres went among the dying with the mercy of the whip and gun. And they closed the cities. They killed ubiquitously, constantly. Two million died along the trails backward leading into the great death pits. One quarter of the gentle land died in those holocaust years, and our Interpreters disdained to inquire of the falling of the shroud that heaved and leaped with the efficient, quick work of the dagger-men of the dream. There was a cartoonist in that time who found rare humor in the tragedy of the gentle land. Thus, the revaluation of compassion.

––––––––

The sky has turned to purple-black outside my eyrie, and the wind has begun again a low wailing. The night increases, deepening over the great headlands and the vast black pools below. Now, the wind's wailing penetrates my chamber, forces itself upon me like an insistent musical discord that some composer of a riven era presents, in its chaotic din, as the theme note of the spinning world, and one must sit and listen to the artist's arrangement of the dissonance arising from the instruments of order and beauty, taking life from the waving wand of the conductor that another time from these same instruments, these same musicians drew forth the sublime song of the Beethoven Ninth. The wailing of the orchestra is rising, and the winds in highest pitch enter the chaos and the wail mounts in shrillness and volume to a screaming that is steady and ceaseless. And there is no respite and no release in the shrieking din, and one wonders how can the orchestra endure, how can the conductor carry further the chaos that is called art because its coded notes lie neatly on and over the musical clef and each instrument joins its sound as it would if commanded to the Ninth, but in the joining of the chaos will the instruments and the players not shatter as the screaming mounts, and heavy droning male tones begin now to dominate the shrieking wail, loud, iron-rasping and louder, bestial overforcing, shattering, destroying, black fire.

———

I am the artist. I am paramount and untranscended. *I am.* My will is power. Value, all order, civility impede my will, I deny them. I shall destroy them. I shall destroy all morality, the very concept of morality. A moral horizon I laugh to scorn. I hate, gloriously: it permits me all things. I suffer no illusion of utopias beyond: I destroy. I am in the service of chaos. My will to power is the will to destroy, to deal death. Death is my beacon. I am the barbarian.

In the blackness that encompasses me, there is no remnant of beauty, of that which was sublime order. To destroy beauty, I have corrupted it. Beauty I have converted to the sensual, and sensual beauty to the erotic, and the erotic to the pornographic. Beauty to filth: that is my sequence. Thus do I disinhibit sensibility for my dagger blows. I am the artist. I am the barbarian.

———

Blackness surrounds me, it is heavy and its force is without surcease, its pain unending, reaching to every point of my being. My screams mock me, echoing with no respite through all the black and hideous night. I do not live — I *am*, only, for there is no light, and life is a touching of the light.

But now, in my chains of knives in the compound of hideousness, I recall the light. I remember the streaming light, the fire of the world golden over its green depths and silver on the mirror of its seas. I remember the light pink and rosy on the grand cumulus, the light, liquid, pouring over the westward plain.

The light only does not mock me, and with its memory I seek escape from the pit of death. I imagine, when I recall the light that I breathe again the free air of my vision from the pinnacle of the earth, and as I remember the sweetness of the light, its source floods over my wretched being and lifts me to it, illuminating in wonder beams the deep world. And I have known the light.

And now I may sing to you again of the world of light that I knew before the Great Darkening of time, the ever glimmering light that soon will flood the world and extinguish the Hideous Epoch which I have seen. I will tell you how you may take back the Great Darkening and find the Neverending Light.

––––––––

The story of our century is the unshackling of power. But we shall reshackle power and liberate man.

Who has removed the bindings of power? Who has released modernity to its fateful course? Who has made of Prometheus, *Subman* Unbound?

The making of man material only, puppet of physical forces without and within him, introduced the Great Release.

What was the Great Release? It was the dream of man born pure, society his corrupter.

What was the Great Release? It was the dream of man material, the economic cog.

What was the Great Release? It was the dream of man the conditioned animal, instinct's bundle of physical desires.

The Great Release was the release of man from God, from that very bond that made man—in and by the sight of God—individual. The Great Release removed the bond that made all men before God equal, before His Law transcending all law. The Great Release unshackled man from law and reshackled man to power. And the hand that had stretched to touch God drew back to form the clenched fist of power, the bludgeon of the twentieth century, power unshackled from law, the power of the dream. Morality, unbound from law, became a mocking, dancing harlequin, and power conquered in the war for the world.

Let us remember the twentieth century for what it has been: the murder of race, class, creed, and all dissent, the industrialization of killing, the creation of power utter and total. The accession of utopia was the restructuring of human nature in the gas chambers and taiga camps and the endless death pits and the murder of the gentle land.

Let us remember the twentieth century for what it has been: the long march of humanity to history's cruelist hoax—the running-out of the Enlightenment in the universe of Power.

But now, power looked out upon a metallic plain unbroken by any obstacle or defining feature, looked out upon the Great Levelling of man—to Subman. But the vista across the metal plain was to no final horizon of light, but to a darkening horizon where a great curtain hung in shadowed folds beyond which gigantic forces waited heavily in the black night where the orbit of the world was passing into the totalitarian age. The death of God was the death of man. What was history's cruelist hoax? It was the dream of self-perfectible man.

Humanity! I declare to you the Great Recalling of the patrimony of the totalitarian century and the Great Return to the regions of light. We shall reshackle power and liberate man. I declare to you the death of the myth of Overman. I declare to you history's indelible truth, sealed by the holocausts of the dream. I declare to you history's indelible truth of imperfectible man, of man completed only as he touches the world's light. And the world's light is God.

Through the blood mists of the twentieth century, I reveal to you the lie of lightless man. I reveal to you that we are free only as we touch the light that frees us from the will to power of lightless man. Let us reshackle power and liberate man. Let us touch the light, and let it burn in the center of our being. Let us take man down from the crucifix of power. I declare the taking-back of material man. I declare the rejoining of the Light.

————

Thus, the masterwork of Michael Brennen, riven great soul, destroyer and restorer, Michael Brennen, Child of God.

LOVE AND FREUD

All thinking, including the most abstract
and objective, can be shown
to have nonrational sources.

— *Sigmund Freud*

[Freud's too?]

I

FASCINATION, PERPLEXITY AND awe held the mind of Karol Lark on his eve of revelation. To have lived in a time of greatest expectation and to see history's high dream dissipated by contingency's hard, ruling winds. The dramatic note of the image only sharpened Lark's sense of utter and total loss as he sat alone in the library of his house listening to the solace-summons of the *Four Last Songs*.

To see one's life's premise turned upon its head — to be compelled to view with honest eye the most vast change of terrain imaginable. In the settling of the light, all hope remnant in Lark lay in the student's strange call that he had discovered and could make available a journal kept by Lark's lost son.

The student's call from three time zones away, waking him at two a.m., was cryptic, callous and mercenary. He'd found an old box in the closet of a rooming house that belonged to "your dead son," and there was a journal in it. Lark could have it, but he'd have to pay.

"Yes, I'll pay you," Lark said, excited.

"Just bring plenty of money," the student said. "You'll find me in the department. Ask for Ringo." He hung up.

A student named Ringo . . . the course of the culture, the passage of time.

Lark booked the flight, then found the Denikins, Martin and Sonia, through their cell phone number — on an Oregon Trail ride! Which seemed to Lark out of character for a Russian scholar couple. Were the Russians now going through a Wild West craze like the Germans? Lark recalled his blunder into a cowboy bar in Munich with Bettina one night the summer of his Fulbright. Everybody in the place, including the barmaids, was wearing Levi's and Stetsons and leather vests. Some of them even sported chaps and spurs.

The Denikins were glad he could come and see them, and told him where to find the house key. Take Elise's old room, Sonia said. You'll know which one it is. We'll be back the day after you get there.

II

From the parking garage, Lark came down to the street just off the narrow avenue rising to the campus of the university he had departed thirty years ago. In this very street, he had once witnessed a student pursuing along the gutter, with apparent fascination, the destination and not the source of a stream of water. The student was enrolled in Lark's own seminar on the Paris Commune, and Lark had looked away. He was glad that, not yielding to the urgencies of grade-creep at the time, he had given the gravity-discoverer a deserved C-.

Turning into the low canyon of the avenue, he was struck by how junked-up the students' "Left Bank" street had become. Crammed along the sidewalks of its outdoor cafes, shops and bookstores were booths and stands of leather trinkets, bluestone jewelry, dog-eared 1940s comic books, and shiny, cased music discs, probably pirated. Litter and garbage filled the gutters, and a runaway, about fifteen — which sex he couldn't tell — was foraging in a trash basket. The sidewalk underfoot was so black and slick with grime that for a moment Lark feared a classic senior fall. He pictured himself sprawled and gazing up in agony at the passing face-traffic of students and streetpeople, some of the faces ring-pierced and surmounted by scalp spikes and all of them likely to register a blank at a call for a Good Samaritan.

When he came to the T-end of the narrow avenue, he glanced across the motor traffic to the historic plaza with its fountain and backdrop of steps and landings that went up to the administration building — outdoor stage of the 'sixties student revolution. When the light changed, the dog waiting unaccompanied beside him — a big, shorthaired male hound — was the first in the crowd to cross. Following, Lark watched as the hound paused to mark a stack of leaflets at the foot of one of the line of student-manned tables before loping on, ignored, to canine business on campus.

Fervent warning-posters, most hand-lettered, were taped to the tables, where Lark could hear the students challenging and exhorting one another oblivious to a famous scholar emeritus passing among them. (Without undue pride, Lark granted that his work was recognized internationally). The posters hearkened to the planet's dangerous warming, sought condom funding to combat epidemics, and deplored the lethal corporate dumping of biotech-grown "Frankenfood" upon exploited peoples.

Lark recalled the oddly matched warnings and enthusiasms at the same tables thirty years ago: the dangerously cooling planet, a call to sexual liberation — "if it moves, fondle it" — and the industrial world's corporate unconcern for the starving nations — socialist solutions and liberation cadres standing ready with the antidote, violence available where needed. In addition were the Days of Rage handouts to raise people's consciousness to the greed and wiles of The Machine and the Power Structure of racist, fascist, imperialist Amerika whose bombs and napalm were regularly killing and maiming the children of the world, all for profit.

Lark was becoming more and more amazed by how brazenly without warning irony was invading his mind.

III

Ignored as casually as the hound, Lark entered the plaza of the university whose student minds he had played a dedicated part in educating to protest and self-absorption in the era bygone, now romanticized by once-Marxist, now market-prosperous, middle-ageing "baby boomers."

He had known then what his students had not yet

known. It was at the turnstiles and in the lens refractors of art and style that power in the future lay. Only secondarily did it and would it reside in the politics of the process. And whose method of social change had indeed proved out? At this tag-end of the twentieth century, the politics of the utopian dream was shattered. But the style refractors were everywhere, ubiquitous in the academy and the culture, a newly sovereign priestly class commanding a theology of art and ritual of learning that suffered no fools.

In fact, a famous emeritus historian of culture (more famous than Lark himself) had lately been compelled to acknowledge an ongoing, fundamental dismantlement of the deeply riven civilization, an admission cheering to the ears of the new clerisy. He had indeed closed the title of his 500-year survey with the surrender word: decadence.

Lark paused to wonder at the mental rant that had seized him in this plaza of memories. Then he saw the glances the students passing by were throwing at him, and he moved slowly on but unable not to wrestle with the question that he sometimes felt was the fundamental question of his *identity* — Nietzschean keyword to the mindset of this end-time, or not-so-end-time.

That question was: to what degree was he personally responsible for the society's ingrained relativism, the pervading narcissism and the deepening cynicism that he saw everywhere? Lark was the historian whose final book had disavowed history, had joined the chorus and gospel of the imperial self beholden in the universe to nothing and free to redefine and remake human nature.

But the gospel had given no sign of giving birth to a

new humanity. Hadn't man found his radical freedom to be a tinderbox he could not contain? In this best and free-est of times, the intellectual and moral wreckage lay everywhere: a standardless art, a literature that seemed locked in the trivial, a poetry of small moments, a faithless and increasingly environment-centered religion, and a politics of increasing mendacity. The academy was deeply politicized, political correctness everywhere carrying the day. And the science of human life, knowing no bounds, eagerly ascended the Tree of Eden oblivious to what lay coiled in its branches. Lark looked upon a culture that wished — barbarically and gently — to codify prenatal and geriatric killing. Had the reigning Bishop of Rome got it right after all — was it a "culture of death"?

Now Lark felt again the heavy tug of irony upon him like a physical force, as if here upon the plaza of student revolution where the 'sixties had begun, he walked in shoes of metal on a field of magnets. Irony — purgative, or disease, of man?

With a start, Lark realized that he was at the very spot where Jeff had been killed. Simple, gentle Jeff, his one child, conscienceless sacrifice to the catechisms of terror the revolution had fathered, the accidental victim of a violent little Stavrogin who had "confronted The Machine" and shot and killed the Navy recruiter manning a table in the plaza of free speech, also killing the nineteen-year-old student boy who'd tried to stop the fusillade.

As he had through the twenty-five years since Jeff's

death, Karol Lark marshalled all power of will to drive from his mind that event. But today, he did not succeed.

He had liked to say that his father's feeling for Jeff was affection, sentimentality, the social adaptation by which human beings learned to live with one another. He did not allow entry into his mind of the false absolute of love, though he knew empirically that love was incontestably the strongest, transcending force of human feeling and action. It was love that *softened* men and women, channelling human thinking finally and unproductively away from history's great engineering task and into the miasma and vain wish of faith. Lark was resolutely, dogmatically he had to say, *not* a man of faith.

Unlike Martin Denikin, his younger colleague and once his student, whom he liked very much. The Denikins had stayed at the university through all its years of upheaval, mainstays of the Russian history faculty, sending occasional bulletins from the front back east to Lark and Bettina.

"Your problem is the troika, Karol," Martin, an Orthodox believer, had told him. "If you take out one of the horses, it won't pull."

Lark knew that he was talking about faith, hope and love, but the greatest of these is love. That was Martin, and that was Sonia, children of the church of the Third Rome, both themselves children of emigres. "Hope is love's gateway, Karol," Sonia told him. "Faith is opening the gate." Lark wasn't interested in gates. But he had to grant the Denikins hope. Wasn't that why he was here?

The insistence of the plaza held him, Jeff's memory piled atop the drama of the beginnings that he could not, on this odd and improbable hope's errand, let alone.

The lone police car that had blundered onto the campus to make a minor trespassing arrest. The activist cadre surrounding it — prisoner, car, and all — not letting it move. The beautiful folksinger who'd rushed up from a Carmel Valley estate to sing protest to the thousands who paused to hear — stage set for the fiery young orator, son of Hegel, to defy The Machine, the rigged society, corporation-owned and standing on the wrong side of history frustrating the liberation of mankind. The bold occupation of the administration building, the corporate president's very lair, and the sit-ins that brought the police on campus in force, the mass arrests, the Third Reich image gained of an emergent American Police State.

The organizing then of a classic, vanguard Steering Committee. The chain of rallies that followed, their subject unimportant, tactic only to the ultimate goal. Free speech, the Dominican incursion, the Vietnam buildup, the troop trains. Nonviolence to violence, street theater, the staged event for an uncritical press, the instream of apostles and disciples from every collateral cause. And the troubadours and the change it's blowin' in the wind Mrs. Robinson. Tune in and turn off and drop out, make love not war, flower power, mind expansion, Lucy in the sky with diamonds, drugs.

Why hadn't the defenders stepped forward in those years? Lark had been astonished. Where were the anchors in the great leftward lurch of the liberal sensibility? 1968, Year of Upheaval.

The flood of memory seemed now a distant roar, receding in echoes that were harder and harder to decipher the sense and rhythm of.

Where *had* all the flowers gone, these children of Marx so earnestly self-styled — middle-class boys with little beards and Che bravado, and middle-class girls in the costumed overalls of vicarious poverty? Why did the Movement draw in so many pretty girls? Why indeed free-love's ingredient in revolution through all ages?

Where were they now, "our best kids," Lark and his colleagues had liked to call them. The orator, dead at forty in his used-book store. The troop-train agitator, a rich stockbroker. The folksinger, faded and forgotten. The troubadours of peace, travelling between multiple villas, market-rich as kings, singing still in high boy-voices to nostalgia and the next thing along. All failed, all compromised, the dream shattered, the big chill, history blocked, the running-out of the revolution in the blood pools of Cambodia's lethal utopia.

And then, the Polish workers — the *real* "proletariat" — and 1989, the Turning. The losing and the winning of the riven century's highest stakes.

It was now more than clear that the early twenty-first century would not "unfold on socialist terrain" — smug rhetoric of an occasion in the 'seventies by a German Nobel laureate of literature and child in the world of international politics. Even the land of the Great Leap Forward was converting to the free market as fast as it could, not to speak of the Subcontinent, now climbing out of the economic bogs of the worldwide dream. Revolution today was no longer red but green, its self-annointed acolytes speaking now not for the proletariat but for the suffering silent earth.

Lark thought upon the collapsed Wall, the astounding event that foreclosed the dream. Aren't you glad? Martin Denikin had said, his own disbelieving joy at odds with the tone sounding out of the utterly unexpected untoward event that had eroded the life studies of countless Western intellectuals. Lark had rather sympathized with the Berlin girl student who, her regime privileges no longer guaranteed, had told the TV cameras: "There is a saying—Bitte, ich will meine Mauer wieder." —Please, give me back my Wall.

Lark was glad he had had the prescience, with his book on socialism, to get the class diagnostician out of his system early, enabling him to move confidently on to the prophet of psyche, no less a revolutionary.

A figure was approaching him, a student, dark-haired, with a smile that was Jeff's smile! And he pressed something into Lark's hand, something small and metallic—a ring? Then the figure was gone. Lark looked at his empty palm, in which he seemed to see an imprint. Are you all right, the dark-haired boy approaching him said, who wasn't Jeff. Can I help you? No, I'm all right, Lark said as he walked slowly on, passing under the arch of the gateway into the inner yard of the university.

The grimy trashiness of the department's faculty corridor was depressing. It was often slept in by drifting homeless, without department objection, he had heard. No ivory tower here to be sure, just a littered hallway and musical noise coming through one of the closed doors that he thought was probably what they called "Grunge." Try as he did, Lark could not syncopate his thinking to Rock in any of its forms, not to speak of Rap, which turned his brain to jelly.

"Did you bring the money?" the goggle-eyed student who was Ringo said. "I want ten thousand."

"I'll give you twenty-five hundred dollars," Lark countered. That was what he had brought with him. "I don't know what I'm getting."

It was more than enough. The student bolted from the department office, ignoring the ringing phones, and could not return fast enough with the battered cardboard carton, which he pitched at Professor Lark's feet, holding out his hand, which was shaking with anticipation.

Lark paid him. Was there a room, a table he could use? No, the department's closed, Ringo said, picking up the phone receiver and jamming it back on its cradle. I've got places to go. Lark knelt and picked up the carton and carried it out of the building. At the plaza, he hired a student to help him with it to his car.

IV

He had always been good with maps and found his way easily up into the East Bay hills where the Denikins had moved. The steep, winding streets that he climbed, barren of trees and heavily cloaked in white stucco and stone, reminded him of an ancient Italian port village, except that all the houses, behind walls that narrowed the streets down to a single lane in places, were villas and all new. Then he recalled the national news story five years earlier about the disastrous East Bay fires. The Denikins had built their dream home in a new, fire-purged villagescape that, with its circling walls and narrow lanes, had a medieval cast.

They'd given him the gate code and he found the house key and he let himself in to the fore chamber of the Denikins' white castle. Lark was drawn at once by the view through the wide arch to the main room of the house, almost a great-hall in its vertical dimension and with a high window-wall looking westward over the bay and beyond to the white hills of the city. The stunning panorama, only a deceptive cluster from the air as he flew in, was a city-forest of white towers that had been no further along thirty years ago than the planning stage. The view held him for several minutes. Then his eye moved to the sweep of the orange span high above the far ocean gate and to the mountain dominating the northern horizon.

Jeff had called it the mountain of the moon and had begged him to take him there. Lark, busy with the book that he hoped would fundamentally define and ground the modern sensibility, had had no time for his young son's fascination with mountains.

At twelve, Jeff had memorized every west coast peak and range. He'd read about all the Mountain Men, too, Jedediah Smith, Jim Bridger, Colter, Kit Carson. I'll bet I can name more Mountain Men than you can, Father, he'd said, delighted. So what, Lark was curt and had cut his son to the quick. What possible difference does it make to me, to anyone, he'd said. And he had registered at once in the eyes of his son the pain he'd inflicted but could not take back.

He had been angry that year, angry about his first book, on the Paris Commune, cradle of necessity, angry at the tepid congratulation by colleagues who, he knew, would never read it. It was a brilliant book!

Now you've paid your dues, Karol, one fellow had said, meaning history's fore-ordained leftward ratchet. That was all.

Lark had disciplined himself in just a week's time to scotch his colleague's name from his mental directory.

Mysterious, romantic, magical mountains, The Lord of the Rings and the Mountains of Shadow, the Captains of the West and evil Mordor, Jeff's simple mindcast. And his son's religious inclination in spite of the emancipated example set. One year in high school, Jeff had bought home an expensive hardback edition of Mann's *The Magic Mountain*. "That book will be lost on you, Jeff. You'll never read it," he'd said with feeling, looking directly into his son's wide eyes. "Why did you buy it? You'll never read it," he'd said again, angrily. And Jeff had thrown the book across the room, breaking the glass and frame of one of Lark's fine Klimt prints. He'd slapped him then, hard. And Jeff had said, why don't you just kill me, hit me again. And he had, sending his son crying hysterically from the room.

Lark hated the author of *The Magic Mountain*. Not for that book explicitly but for its author's brilliant dissection, in another book, of the mind of the Austrian composer whose theory, early in the century, had eliminated beauty from music. Modelled on that composer, the Nietzschean musician of Mann's *Doktor Faustus* had essayed a self-destroying "taking back" of the sublime beauty of Beethoven's great Ninth Symphony.

The Austrian's "anti-music", whose deconstructing intent Mann had so clearly penetrated and depicted, had been a trumpet call to the newer world. Now, at the turn of the millennium, no one listened anymore to the great composer of pure reason's non-beauty, while the Ninth Symphony was as beloved of audiences as two hundred years before.

Against those reactionary countercurrents of the century, Lark had brought to completion the great book of his career, the historian's grail, key to modernity itself. With that book, he believed he had come closer than had anyone to documenting, dramatizing the birth of the modern world in its great creative burst in Europe's cities of light. On the book's brilliance, his readership agreed, and on its influence to come. I'm proud of you, Father, Jeff had said, and Lark remembered he'd been amused by that, making no reply, and in that silence, Jeff had dropped his eyes.

The book was his credential, his permanent pass to the sedate, prestigious banks of the Charles, a continent distant from the more and more violent battlescape left behind in the painful drawdown years and the denouement of Vietnam. Jeff did not come east with them, choosing to stay and study literature in the combat zone Lark was glad to abandon.

And yet, was not the grand palace empty? A profound sense of failure gripped the historian of heroic modernism. There had been a downside to his transfer, Marx to Freud. A descent was apparent from the apex of high rational- ity onto the inchoate and jumbled terrain of the irrational. Didn't the cratered landscape, with all its little rainpools of self and no drainage pattern apparent, mean the sus- pension of any universal order, even of history itself?

Hadn't the descent proved terminal, in fact? One of the problems was that most of the poolets of self, from which insight was expected, were stagnant tarns. A more seri- ous problem was that, by the doctrine of the imperial self, no authority could exist to prefer the insights of one pool over those of another. Finally, since all thought was the conditioned product of the irrational ruling subconscious, including the theoretical system of its founding father, that system itself had logically to surrender its claim to universal validity.

Karol Lark confronted the fin-de-siecle's ineluctable disarraying truth: the whole spiral of the modernist faith was downward. The failure that had devastated the lib- erationist academy was a wider failure, sweeping away the liberator of psyche as well. Art, music, poetry, litera- ture, politics, fallen false morality — what in the twentieth century had not owed and paid tribute to the Founder through whose body of ideas Lark had strained the bright particularites of his own — many said brilliant — scholarship to produce his bestseller.

All about him and within him, Lark knew, was the order of nature, the world and the universe in its fantastic intricacy and its dynamic, stupefying immensity. Here, at the tag end of the century, at the outset of an unknown millennium, the patent falsity of the great belief system in which his life's scholarship and reputation were vested, fell upon him like a torrent.

Lark looked clearly into the hollowed-out heart of the brave new world now dying. How very much did the receding materialist faiths of modernity resemble the arcane and guarded codexes of the ancient Egyptian priests. The final big chill was the chill of the emptied, bare and ruined temple of the secular church. The heart of modernism, generating its own fatal disease, had stopped beating.

V

Lark turned from the window and went to forage in the Denikins' kitchen for some bread and cheese and beer. Locating Elise's room up one flight, he got his bags and then brought up the box, which he set down beside the wide teak desk that looked out, like the living room below, to the bay and the city.

The room was unmistakably female furnished. But his eye was drawn to its paintings and prints, what were they? Elise's parents' Russian icons, and prints of paintings of saints and reformers, religious landscape themes, including a cross in a misty German mountainland, which

Lark recognized as a product of the Dresden School. On the dresser was a framed photograph, and Lark lifted it to the light.

Posed with her parents, the Denikins' adopted daughter had now to be, Lark calculated, twenty-three or -four. Elise was blonde, pretty and poised, looking confidently at the camera and the world. She had large eyes, their upper line slightly "isosceles". Like Jeff's, he realized — his own, too.

Elise was an Episcopal priest. Why is she studying theology, he'd asked Martin when he'd seen the Denikins at a conference several years ago. She discovered Niebuhr, Martin answered. Ah, yes, Lark mused. The traitorous theologian, early herald of the church's Marxian reform, but all too briefly in the accumulating crisis of the 'thirties. *The Nature and Destiny of Man.* But had Niebuhr not been right after all: that man could not handle his radical freedom alone?

Lark now turned to Jeff's box, taking out the journal and looking only briefly at the further contents. Here were Jeff's Boy Scout treasures — his merit badge sash, an old khaki-colored flashlight, a scout knife, his Eagle Scout medal. And his little collection of porcelain and wood-carved dogs. Lark and Bettina had not let him have a dog or any pet, and after he had cried he'd finally said to them: I'll just get dog statues then. And Jeff's "mountain books." Lark opened one, its pages underlined: *The Magic Mountain.*

Their flight out, when the news came, had been an ordeal, Bettina beside him, not saying a word, but neither had he. What was his wife thinking, this most politics-centered woman he had ever known, capable of extended rants and rhetorics at mere mention of the foe. Bettina had grown up in the storied radical high school in Manhattan and in one of those New England summer colonies where the neighbors of her famous theologian father sometimes sheltered radical young men thought to be under F.B.I. surveillance, one of whom had been her first.

And Lark had been her last, she choosing him, at a library table the year he'd begun his dissertation. She had even planned their honeymoon trip to her revolutionary-romantic taste. Where? he'd asked, astonished. What? To the Finland Station!? And they had seen "the future that worked," and though they'd found Leningrad austere and unnecessarily restrictive, they had understood history's necessity: one cannot make an omelette without first breaking eggs — in a famous formulation.

They had sat a few minutes, both silent, after the call came, Bettina crying, but not Lark. What was a child? A little human being we can never know, an impermanent personality passing from infant to adult, a stranger who enters and leaves our lives. Jeff was their biological contribution. He had said these things before, but he did not say them now.

But neither had she wanted to bring a child into the soiled world of the utterly unnecessary Cold War, sparked by Truman, deepened by Eisenhower. When Jeff came anyway, Bettina had gotten a nanny, though they couldn't really afford it then, to help out and to keep the place quiet. Yet, Jeff was so endearing, seeking their affection—Lark abjured "love", sun-word of sentimentality and false morality. And yet, his son's spontaneous feeling had staggered him: Jeff did not want to play with blocks and puzzles, but with blocks and puzzles *with him.*

Jeff had insisted on "love" anyway. "I love you, Father," he'd say without prologue or warning. "Yes, yes," Lark replied. "But call me Daddy." "No, you are Father. I love you, Father." "All right," Lark said.

Our "love" child, he told Bettina.

"There's a saying," he said to his son in the presence of friends when Jeff was six, in order to properly instruct him. "There's a saying: act your I.Q."

"We like you Jeff, very much," he'd added to assure him.

"I call it love," Jeff said, happy.

Lark had gotten it over with as quickly as possible, though the Denikins, devout believers, had intervened and taken over. "There will be a church service," said Sonia, who had tutored Jeff in Latin. "I loved Jeff." They had looked after all the arrangements.

"Our love child, our stranger," Bettina said oddly on the return flight.

"No more complications, Karol," she added. "No more interruptions to the Enlightenment Project."

He was used to the sarcasms, but when he looked her in the face, he saw only grief.

When they got back, she moved out. Soon after the settlement, he heard that she was sick, and he called. But she wouldn't see him. When Bettina died, the Denikins came to help out, and Lark was grateful.

VI

Karol Lark began to read the journal of his son, the school-boy's print familiar and neat, every letter legible. The entries were dated, sporadic and, he soon saw, self-confiding.

There was a first entry about the Mountain. Against the late afternoon sun, Lark looked out over the bay and its islands to the peak looming in the northern sky. I love my Holy Mountain, Jeff wrote. Lark remembered.

As he read into the second page and the third, he realized that he was holding in his hands the confessional of Jeff's soul. The sensation came to Lark suddenly that, out of the neat lettering of this document, his son was speaking to him, as if a spirit were palpable on the page. Now, he placed the journal flat upon Elise's desk, drew his hands away from it to rid himself of the attack of superstition.

But in this, he did not fully succeed. The journal, in neat script — no cross-throughs, no scratchings-out — was speaking to him. And Lark had again to look up and see the panorama of the white towers of the city to break the spell, to assure himself that what he was registering was not in some inexplicable way aural and not visual only.

From the high window of Elise's castle chamber, the gateway, in the rapidly passing minutes, took on its golden sheen. Lark's far vision had never lost its acuity, and he could see again, even above the brilliant reflection of the sea gate, the orange sweep of the fabled span. And his eye shifted once more to the now darkening hulk in the north, Jeff's Mountain.

He looked again to the document lying before him and now he suddenly willed his hands to touch it and hold it. His scholar's practice asserted itself, and as he listened to and read intensively each page, a frame of classification imposed itself upon his mind.

Jeff's entries were falling into three main subjects: the Mountain and all that reminded him of it—Ararat, and Moses' mountain, and Petrarch's and, yes, the magic mountain of the seeker Hans Castorp, the early penetrating vision of the century's unfolding fierce and fatal contradictions.

And . . . a girl named Joyce.

Jeff's third subject, Lark recognized, with physical shock, was Lark himself!

The entry appeared again and again: Child of my Father. Father, Father, I love you, I love you Father, Father, Father, Father, Father.

Karol Lark began to weep, as he had not since his own college freshman year, when he had faced his aloneness in the fearful world and the pointless universe. And before he could move to prevent it, his tears fell on the journal page, staining and running the neatly inked letters by which his son was talking to him over the echoing chasm of twenty-five years. For the first time in his life of mind, Lark experienced the jolting fusion of pain and joy.

An awareness of where he was and why now fell away to the intensity of his reading. He read quickly, memorizing without trying every paragraph and page, as he had one spectacular graduate year of unbroken honors grades.

And so he read, sometimes hardly breathing, of

Ossian's hill of storms and of the cross in the mountains of Caspar David Friedrich, and of Joyce who had told him her name was from the Bretagne. What was it? His son's neat print had only made comment that God had done his best work among the Celtic-French.

Joyce was a runaway, an orphan, "my precious little wife to be," Jeff wrote. "I am your mountain, little Joyce, your warm cave in the hill of storms."

Joyce was seventeen, and Joyce would have a baby.

For the second time this night in the high castle, Karol Lark was struck to the quick.

Now, he quickly turned the page, recognizing at once by the date that he had reached the journal's end.

I will marry her, and I will be Father now, and I will love my Child! My Child! My Child! My Child! My Child! . . . . The entry repeated for two full pages.

Lark slumped, exhausted, in the desk chair.

But there had been no Joyce, no young girl there when they'd buried Jeff, only the Denikins and a couple of Jeff's professors. Why?

A young girl alone, pregnant, grief-stricken, shattered?

He did not sleep, and the next morning, before meeting the Denikins, as arranged, in the city, he went to the county courthouse and surveyed a two year tally of birth records. Not one unmarried mother Joyce listed, father known or unknown.

VII

For the Denikins, it was Good Friday. They came directly from the airport to meet Lark at the cathedral. It's Elise's first high communion they'd said.

They were waiting for him at the great bronze doors, Martin and Sonia, and he was glad to see them. They went through the portal and the antechambers and into the high nave. You could call the Gothic cathedrals of the New World imitations if you wanted to, Lark thought, but they weren't. Every one that he had seen in the world was unique, its own gallery of glass and stone carving set in soaring interior space.

The wastage of space! But he could no longer say that as he once had. Didn't all the modern galleries, the odd barn-like boxes that seemed angled and faceted at whim, the double cylinders and the triangle assemblages of the modern age, didn't they all follow the Gothic in their demand for light and height? Though, of course, someone was always hanging a mobile in the vastness of the inner space, which took your eye off the inadvertent industrial plainness.

The Gothic cathedral — engineering marvel of the pre-industrial world, unequalled in its aesthetic concentration and its mystic capture of the human eye. The Denikins led the way up the wide central aisle, and they found seats only a dozen rows back, from where you could see all the rich detail of the holy day mass.

Lark studied the high windows, in which he, the art historian, knew every figure and symbol. But these he passed over in order to admire the tapestried brilliance of the whole. When he looked down again, the church had filled, and the robed procession, crucifer, acolytes and choirboys, had begun. With Martin and Sonia, he turned and watched them approaching, innocents on the cusp of the light-dark world. They were singing, sweet boy voices, sweet sons — great gift, great fortune.

Over the procession flowed the beautiful paired solos of the Vivaldi *Laudamus Te*, which, for its ascent to the sublime, Lark had never been able to dismiss from his unbelieving mind. "Disarming, isn't it," Sonia whispered to him wickedly.

"Here's Elise now," she nudged him at the approach of the procession of the canons and auxiliary priests. In the richly robed ranks of her bearded, bespectacled and bald pated colleagues, Elise looked like a bright angel descended — he couldn't help himself.

She had long, wheaten hair, reminding him of Bettina's, and she was beautiful. "Our angelic daughter," Martin, who stood on Lark's other side, said, reading his thoughts. "Like a Russian beauty."

Lark agreed. "You two have me entrapped," he said. "And entranced."

"You've entranced yourself," Sonia said.

They prepared for the rite of communion. As the rows of churchgoers went forward, Lark saw that Elise's function was the chalice, though they also had little tumbler trays of wine. "Come with us," Sonia said. "It'll do you good."

"You know I can't," Lark told her.

"Oh, come on anyway. Just fake it."

Surprised to find himself stepping into the aisle, he followed Sonia and Martin to the rail. He surprised himself again as he knelt, for the first time since childhood. In the efficiency of the liturgy, Elise was before them almost at once, beaming at her parents. And as she pressed the cup upon him, Lark looked up into her eyes, so beautifully shaped, lightly "isosceles." She returned his look of surprise with her own, then passed on and down the rail.

How exactly did you come to find Elise, he asked them that evening. We were in Carmel early one morning, Martin told him. We were at the Mission just as it opened. They'd found a baby girl, newborn, and her mother, too. She was very young. Someone had brought them to the Mission and left in a hurry. But the mother died before the ambulance came. Whoever had helped her with the birth did something wrong. There were hippie colonies and communes in the mountains back then. Maybe that's where they brought her from. Lark remembered the fabled Bay to Big Sur pilgrimage, the ubiquitous hippie vans, almost every one of them an old, beat-up Volkswagen decorated with peace symbols and flower decals and crammed with innocents, and not so innocents, lost.

"There was nothing to identify her," Martin said. "All there was was a ring. She was buried as a Jane Doe."

"We asked to adopt. The court gave us Elise."

"God gave us Elise," Sonia said.

"Yes," Martin said.

"Elise puts flowers on her mother's grave," Sonia added. "She goes down to Carmel several times a year."

"What happened to the ring?" Lark asked.

"We got it. We gave it to Elise when we told her. It's in the jewelry box in her desk."

"What kind of ring was it?" Lark said.

"It was just a boy's ring, a Boy Scout ring."

"I'd like to see it," Lark said after a moment, not able to disguise the huskiness in his voice.

He looked at once inside the band to find the letters Jeff had scratched in it when he was thirteen: J E D. Jedediah Smith, Jeff's Mountain Man hero.

"Resurrection," Sonia said, after a moment, when he told them on this eve of the highest holy day, Eastern and Western Church. And he let them read the journal of the Child of My Father.

"It's for his child, and yours, to keep," he said. "But a grandfather would like to come and read it sometimes."

"She will read it with you," Martin smiled.

"Will she love me?"

"Didn't Jeff?" Sonia said.

Through all the night of Karol Lark's day of revelation, slumbering in his granddaughter's darkened room, he opened his eyes from time to time and saw, but did not wonder at, the light that seemed everywhere around him.

THE MYSTERIOUS STRANGER

. . . the report of my death was an exaggeration.

— Mark Twain

The times were strange, they were not as they seemed. The reappearance on earth of the famous author ninety years after his passing could not have happened. And yet, do a thousand cameras lie? Must we not conclude that the strange visitation of the in-the-flesh spirit of the intractable Mr. Clemens did indeed occur? The event was mystifying, the fact of it bewildering. What interrogative exists to apply to the sightings reported worldwide in the final cycle of our old 20th century as the world approached the midnight of the millennium?

I

THE FIRST SIGHTINGS took place where you might expect they would. On an early morning, a caretaker's boy saw him, white-maned and moustached, wearing his trademark white linen suit, climbing through the window of the two-room cabin where he was born. Nobody in Florida, Missouri or anywhere else believed the boy's tall tale until the noon incident in Hannibal a day later generated the first news story.

In Tom Sawyer's old St. Petersburg, they had hired a spirited, white-coiffed actor to saunter the streets dressed like Twain to entertain the tourists. When the Twain imitation spotted a rival look-alike gazing across Main Street at the boarded-up windows of the Mark Twain Hotel, his saunter quickened. Thunder in his outrage, he accosted the interloper. Witnesses who were thought to be reliable saw it all.

Tapped hard on the shoulder by the indignant Hannibal employee, the stranger turned on his heel, looked his impersonator up and down, and said in a voice that carried: "Get out of that ridiculous costume before I tear it off your worthless carcass!" Twain grabbed his stand-in by the lapels and shook him violently. The city's employee swooned and collapsed from agitation and the noon heat. Bending over his imitator, Twain advised: "The report of my death was an exaggeration," — adding with his fabled pithiness: "Thunder is impressive; but it is lightning that does the work."

Around Hannibal after that, you saw him often — wandering the tiny rooms of his boyhood home, once stretching out, hands behind his head, on his quilted bed; or inspecting Becky Thatcher's house across the street; or at the board fence the tourist children come to whitewash every summer and where he took up a brush for a few licks of his own.

Soon other sightings occurred around the state. From the cobbles of the St. Louis riverfront, an early riser saw him standing under the great Gateway Arch watching the reflected dawn descend the silvered span, apogee to earth. On a country music stage in Branson, the stranger in white silenced all sound, voice and stringed instrument, in an act duplicating his fabled stage appearances of a hundred years before. Coming out of the wings, the beloved gadfly walked slowly across the stage, pausing every few feet to turn and gaze and scowl in comic disbelief at his amused audience. "I thought man couldn't be any worse," he told them. "Until I got sight of you. Be warned: heaven goes by favor. If it went by merit, you would stay out and your dogs would go in."

After that, the mysterious stranger was seen at the wheel of the *Delta Queen* plying Twain's Mississippi, shoving the pilot roughly aside and muttering to himself about the unfamiliar, unresponding steering mechanism. At a Confederate reenactment of the Marion Rangers, and on the waterfront in San Francisco, in Virginia City, in Elmira, Heidelberg and Rome—wherever he had lived and travelled—Twain put in an appearance, astonishing all witnesses.

As the sightings multiplied, dozens of cameras and TV lenses began to record the famous image. But when an aggressive reporter approached the figure and attempted to touch, or perhaps grab, him, the author of "The Celebrated Jumping Frog" dissolved and vanished, advising as he disappeared: "Stick to your scribbling!"

Children, however, he allowed to touch his coat or shake his hand, softening his customary fierce gaze when they did. But other, adult contact incidents were less happy. One of these was the ringing slap across the face the stranger administered to a surprised Twain biographer he encountered in the stacks of the university's Mark Twain Collection at Berkeley. The assault brought on precinct-station belly laughs when the abused academic tried to file charges.

Often the cameras and camcorders captured a singular expression in the unmistakable physiognomy of Samuel L. Clemens—spirit or spirit re-embodied or magician or whoever this most inexplicable filmed and witnessed apparition was. Whether standing or walking or sitting at rest, usually with a cigar in hand, Twain levelled at the lens the sober and fierce take-no-prisoners gaze beloved of six admiring generations going on seven.

Soon forensic photography experts took note of the mystery figure and subjected their photo images to the scrutiny of end-century technology. Twain had posed and sat for scores of photographers. Placed against those historical images, the visitor's visage matched them exactly in every measurable detail. Beyond the white, unruly hair and bristly eyebrows and the drooping moustache that identified him instantly the world over, the forensics men nailed down an exactitude of feature impossible to alter by any would-be Twain of the species: the aquiline nose and strong chin, the brow, furrowed in late age, the crow-feet lines of kindness in the humor-creased face, the eyes that reflected the transcendent humanity that drew affection the world over.

The eye of Mark Twain came under particular study. No imitator's eye, not even that of his best impersonator, Hal Holbrook, could match the spark of light that flashed in every image old and new, as if from Pindar's own command to turn the brightness outward. Twain's eye, then and now, saw through to the human heart at once, missed nothing. Alternately fierce and kind, the eye in the dead-pan face of the matchless student of mankind was never not inquisitive and bright, or dimmed by time. Mark Twain's eyes could not know tranquility, neither did the stranger's.

As weeks passed, the scenes of the visitation were no longer limited to places Twain had known in his comet-crossed life. He was observed walking the grounds at Flossenbuerg, where the martyred German Resistance pastor, Dietrich Bonhoeffer, was hanged by the Nazis in the last days of the Second World War. In a garden over-looking the River Volga, he surprised the laureate Russian novelist and historian of the Soviet Gulag Archipelago, Aleksandr Solzhenitsyn.

He appeared in scores of other chosen places. Outraging its custodian, Twain entered the sacrosanct, dusty stacks of the poet Goethe's library, still intact in the Weimar house of the German Enlightenment's central figure. Later the same day, observers saw him studying the grim monu-ment reminders of the Buchenwald concentration camp in the nearby hills. Out of nowhere, he appeared, wear-ing a surgeon's gown, in a Boston women's clinic. "O, you damned angels of mercy!" His shout rattled the surgeon and the nurses. "If I were superintending the rain," they heard him quietly say after a moment, "I would rain softly and sweetly on this poor child. But I would drown you."

II

Accusatory theories inevitably surfaced. Responsible Journalism initially dismissed the sightings as hoaxes and copycat stunts, multiplied by tabloid fabrications. As the sightings continued, however, crowd psychology and mass hysteria theories emerged to explain the phenomenon. Then, as the tide of reliably witnessed incidents swelled, conspiracy conjectures took center stage.

The conspiracy theories surrounding the return of Mark Twain to walk the earth in the year 1999 at mankind's turn to the third millennium, A.D. followed patterns common to the times. Thus, the theories were factually imaginative, bizarre, and sold books, some scholarly.

The theories extracted flashes and gems of genius from the literary over- and nether-world. "Traditionalist, Snopesist recrudescence" was posed as a leading probability explaining the spirit sightings of Clemens the semi-southerner. The Mark Twain impersonations were seen to be "spontaneous irruptions on the moribund body of traditional literature in terminal autosuffocation by 'values'." Less intellectually weighty was a theory that the backwaters and benighted regions had produced, in the hapless Twain look-alikes, a second generation of failed Elvis wannabes.

Paleoconservatism had again come out from under its rock, as it was so often lately doing, in order to secretly train a battalion of Twains to "nostalgia-ize" the nation and thereby distract and stultify the advancing literary taste—deflecting the culture from metafiction, minimalism, chicklit, and other expressions of the ongoing literary flowering. It was significant that both Richard Nixon and Ronald Reagan had admired Mark Twain. A serious haberdashery historian warned that the neat white suits represented "an arrogant (if laughable) attempt to reimpose bourgeois dress values", moreover providing aid and comfort to "the elitist literary dinosaur Tom Wolfe—he of copycat Twain costumery." Not only an egregious social evil but an encouragement to global warming were manifest in the air polluting cigars the battalion of Twains were invariably seen enjoying.

Discomfiting and reassuring as these theories were to writerly sensibilities, they did not satisfy the general public. People remained baffled and fascinated by the continuing appearances. One might understand a Twain visit to the New York tomb of U.S. Grant, the Union general he had admired and entertained and whose memoir publication he had assisted. But now, increasingly, the figure began to be sighted at war markers of the 20th century—at Arlington and Normandy and at the great war cemeteries in Luxembourg and Lorraine and at many unmarked places, once violent now tranquil, across the globe, whose locations he sought out.

III

The amazing and inexplicable incidents acquired a dimension more bizarre and perplexing with the book vandalizings.

Perhaps the mystery returnee—Mark Clemens or Sam Twain or whoever he was taken to be, spirit or hoax or gadfly conspiracy—had been set off by the vast fields and sites of war and genocide he visited. Soon after these worldwide sightings took place, the apparition began to appear, almost exclusively, in libraries and in bookstores, startling the browsers, students, and store and library staffs as he took down bound volumes of his own great oeuvre from the stacks and stands.

Crowds were always gathering now, though he seldom paid them any attention. His captivated watchers knew better than to intrude and precipitate a vanishing act. As Twain leafed through an edition of *Innocents Abroad* or *Pudd'nhead Wilson*, his impromptu audiences saw him occasionally smile, or they heard a muttered affirmation such as: "Yes, yes, I put that just right," or "I'd say the same thing again." But the photos and footage of these incidents also recorded fierce scowls — and worse.

The vandalizings occurred invariably when he drew down an edition of one book in particular, the title of which, if not its sober content, was known to every card-clutching child familiar with "Authors". *The Mysterious Stranger*, Twain's final major work, was a bitter compendium of the religious skepticism of the author and his times, uncertain era of the melancholy roar of receding faith and certitude. In consternation, the silent well-wishers watched Twain remove from his coat pocket an old fashioned pen and, upon the page margins of the fiction tract that depicted his Mysterious Stranger's portrayal of a frivolous, cruel God, scratch angry exclamations.

"No! No! No! Ridiculous! Utterly wrong!!" the violent scrawls read. "What a fool!! Why did I say that?!"

Upon Twain's sudden departures following these visits, his witnesses leaped to seize the now priceless vandalized copies.

"Illusion? Illusion? How could I have written that

jackassery — 'everything is illusion'?" This scratched entry appeared on the page of a valuable early edition, to the horror of its custodian. "The author has boiled himself to death in his own bile." Twain wrote alongside the text of his often cited cynicism that man "begins as dirt and departs as stench."

These baffling, violent notations, an attack by Twain's ghost on the writer's own savaging of "the Moral Sense" and its claimant vehicle, the Church, sent several Twain scholars specialized in his late, "dark" period, into high orbit. And when an eminent endowee of an ivied institution lost control and rushed to jerk away the vandalizing hand, Twain responded with an assault requiring a 9-1-1 call. "Some Saducees would interrupt the raising of Lazarus," he commented as the scholar was carried out.

Even stranger than the depredations on the rare editions and paperbacks of *The Mysterious Stranger* were the "kneeling" incidents that followed.

Chronicler of the foibles and foolishness of church-going mankind, the famous skeptic who had let his own Mysterious Stranger, Satan, have the last word, next put in an appearance on a Sunday morning in the great nave of the National Cathedral before several hundred worshippers. No camcorders were on hand to record the unlikely sighting, but the stunned attendees all gave the same account.

Slowly down the long central aisle of the great Gothic cathedral walked the author of *What is Man?*, gazing at the high, stained-glass window walls, his figure the cynosure of every astonished eye but the organist's, and then of his

too, so that an awed silence followed the step of the latter day mysterious stranger down the nave of the house
of belief. Reaching the crossing of the high transepts, he
ascended the steps to the choir of the church and, before a
great Christian cross, dropped to his knees and appeared
silently to pray.

This act, uncharacteristic of the living author whose
life of adventure and unsurpassed literary fame was en-
cyclopedically recorded and was the subject of a thousand
graduate studies, was duplicated in other worship houses
grand and humble. He was seen in the great cathedral in
Cologne, and at teeming St. Peter's where, in his angel-
white livery, the crowds parted before him as if suddenly
confronted with a rival American pope. There were sightings at the Church of the Holy Sepulcher, at a storefront
sanctuary in Erie and in a Lutheran church in Columbia,
Missouri.

In all these appearances, the camrecorded or flash-
bulbed image was the same: Twain's fierce, withering
stare below the bushy white eyebrows of a head bowed,
a stare that froze the step of any minister, parishoner, or
tourist so foolish as to try to say hello.

At the location which would register as the final appearance of the ghost who visited the world of 1999 — the
Chapel of Four Chaplains in Philadelphia — the fabled
fierceness dropped away. Those present in the memorial church honoring the chaplains, Protestant, Catholic
and Jew, of the torpedoed troopship *Dorchester,* who had
calmed the chaos, then given their places in the lifeboats
to four young sailors and gone down with the ship — these

witnesses saw tears spring from the eyes of the caustic critic of the "damned human race."

IV

The visitation ended as abruptly as it had begun. A week, then another, passed without a sighting. At the end of the second week, seven American newspapers received an unusual, lengthy letter, multi-addressed. As it turned out, the recipient in each case was a newspaper extant or descending from a paper in print in Twain's time, some of which he had written for. The letter, typed on an ancient machine with ribbon-blackened a's and o's, bore the signature, "Theodor Fischer."

The letter's length and unknown signer resulted in the copies being initially laid aside — all but one. The editor of the Hannibal, Missouri *Courier-Post*, who had himself seen and reported the Twain apparition, recognized the sender's name: the boy narrator of *The Mysterious Stranger*. The signature seemed to resemble Twain's peculiar scrawl and was either authentic or a good forgery. Later handwriting analyses tended to support the former.

What measures of plausibility can one rely on in times that are strange and things are not as they seem? Sam and Orion Clemens' news successor in Mark Twain's Hannibal assessed the chances and published his scoop. The mysterious stranger in the land of the living at the end of the 20th century at the dawn of a new millennium presented the answer to the riddle of his strange visitation:

A Letter to the Damned Human Race

I did not expect to see Halley's Comet a third time — from any vantage, earth, heaven, or hell. Was not everything under Satan's sun, the orb of my mysterious stranger Phillip Traum, an illusion? God, and Satan too, and life itself or, as your century's lifeless word has it, 'existence' — a word that strikes me as a little like whiskey with the alcohol extracted — was not everything after all an illusion? That is what I told you in my final manuscript, when my comet came to take me — to oblivion, I thought — although I was still not quite sure about it, superstition gripping me sometimes. As Halley's fireball streaked above me, I said to my daughter, my sweet Clara, "Maybe I will see you again."

But I confess I was flabbergasted — to a state of utter stupefaction — by my posthumous trip and journey's end. And as I quickly found out — for apostasy, penance was due, even for someone with my sweet disposition. "You are a hard case, Sam, worse than a mule," the Creation Authority told me. "We are sending you back for reconsideration. A new century and millennium are coming. Go and see what happened, Long Ears, to the 'Moral Sense' you took us so severely to task for, you undevout droll and scalawag. Back to Earth with you, and Godspeed!"

Well, where had I thought humor came from?

Fossils? The rocks? By the way, They have for-
given Mr. Darwin his brilliant error. They told me
no mortal gazing through the bottle-glasses of the
time could have known how intricate They had
made the living cell, such that a random change to
a part of it would pulverize it, not improve it. But I
leave that argument for your age to wrestle to honest or dishonest conclusion.

First, to what I have learned from my privi-
leged revisit.

I believed, when I departed the earth in 1910,
that our religion was our prison. I had thought all
the world's competent killers were Christian. I said
so as forcefully as I thought I could get by with.
Isn't everyone a moon, and has a dark side which
he never shows to anybody?—though I did—I
knew my readers would forgive much to the creator of Tom Sawyer and Huckleberry Finn.

My final earthly testament was Phillip Traum's
visit to the Austrian village of "Eseldorf". This
much, some of you might remember. In my fable,
I tore the wings off angels, for my innocent little
schoolboys and for all in posterity who would lend
an ear to my fable.

But I know, from my current time with you, of
another Austrian schoolboy for whom the mind-
molders of the 20th century had torn off the angels'
wings. (I observed in my tour of the German lands
that "Adolf" has since dropped from preferred lists
of boys' names). And I know of the Russian school-

boys around whose little heads the good angels were no longer flying, as they imbibed of the wisdom of a material world desiring to hammer mankind on the anvil of perfectibility. Mr. Solzhenitsyn had the definitive history of that, which he made me read along with Ivan Denisovich, while serving me tea and a good vodka.

Some people were born calm, I was born excited. So now, as I tear the wings off your angels, hold fast! . . . Though you are in luck. I have kept my sense of humor—just barely, you blind and self-damned horde, hopeless Jackass Race that only a Creator could love and want to justify. Let me say this: my innocents abroad were naive and foolish. But they were innocent. Not one of my pilgrim shipmates to Rome and Jerusalem could have imagined Buchenwald or the Gulag, or any of the horrors inflicted by the archdemons your new world unleashed. My Satan Traum pales by comparison.

I ask you: How did the century I left behind achieve such things? Apparently there is nothing that cannot happen.

It is evident you are dolts. To what piper's envy-tune did you crowd like children into the beckoning caverns of your lethal utopias? How could you have taken seriously the specious science of chance? A chance designer of nature's fantastic intricacy? A chance physicist of the grand cosmos and its astonishing mathematical tolerances? You are numbskulls and not only sinners. One day, just a little curious, I happened into a "playboy mansion". What I saw would drive a saint to weep and a pig to blush. What led you, you lunatics, to become 'libido'-driven hedonists? And what cretin invented "situation ethics"? Situational betrayal? Situational rape? Situational infanticide? What happened to satire — and common sense? Your era cries for both. But that would require the dolt to activate his brain.

At the midnight of the millennium, as I await my departure, I listen with you to the Ode to Joy choruses circling the globe. "Alle Menschen werden Brueder." In our brilliant and violent century you have achieved the opposite of brotherhood. Why? You believed me — consequently you believed in much less. You demoted God, like a good tooth fairy, to an invention of man and elevated yourselves — you supposedly hapless products of blind material forces — to the highest moral authority. You filled God's vacuum with all too "human" creeds, with God pretenders who seized whole nations and eliminated the unwanted and the inferior by the scores of millions. No effective remnant of the "Moral Sense" I disparaged survived in those places to say *No! No! No!* I cry now for the angels wings. I weep for my schoolboys.

You may disbelieve my visitation to your world and judge it, too, a strange and passing illusion (though the "Twain scholars" whose ears I enjoyed boxing will remember it differently). You may hold to your blindness that this is all there is, that we are the chance interplay of matter and nature only. Will my visit disabuse you of that confusion, you idleheads? Can a cat be bathed? But I pose to all my fellow Long Ears, a question you cannot dismiss:

Out of what earthly material urge could the four chaplains have acted as they did? Go see their shrine (possibly the only holy place left on earth). Was their act not an echo of another, greater Act, the signal event of all history, forward time, and reality? What was the crux of that other Great Act, its be-all and end-all?

I did not expect to encounter the world of Grace my comet brought me to, the world whose matchless gift lies beyond nature, matter, comets and stars, and of which word speaks. I did not deserve the admission ticket, as do none of us. But wasn't my Tom after all a hymn, like I said he was, and warn't Huck my very own soul? So I return now to the Other Side, humbled and hopeful. But for insurance I'm going back with a restless frog in my pocket.

Safe Waters to you,
"Theodor Fischer"

ABOUT THE AUTHOR

NICKELL JOHN ROMJUE, a historian and writer, was born in Washington, D.C. and grew up in Macon, Missouri. He served in the Cold War U.S. Army in Germany and studied modern European history and German literature at the universities of Missouri, California-Berkeley, and Heidelberg as a Fulbright Scholar. He is the author of books about late-20th century American military doctrine and forces, including *The Army of Excellence, From Active Defense to AirLand Battle,* and *American Army Doctrine for the Post-Cold War.* His fiction stories, which have received national and regional awards, have appeared in *The Missouri Review, Shenandoah, The South Dakota Review, Sou'wester* and many literary journals, and his stories, articles, and history and fiction reviews have been published in over thirty magazines and newspapers as well as in European publications. He is the author of two fiction collections, *Out of the Riven Century: Stories of a Turning Time* (2001), and *Witches of Devon: Tales of the Humorous and Strange* (2002), and a short novel, *Merry Town, Missouri - 1945-1948* (2005). He is a past member of the board of governors and past first vice president of the Virginia Writers Club, and his publications have been noted in *Who's Who in America* and *Who's Who in the World*. He lives with his wife Inge in Yorktown, Virginia, and is the father of two children.

Printed in the United States
107340LV00002B/228/A